BBC
DOCTOR WHO

THE
MISSY
CHRONICLES

BOOKS

1 3 5 7 9 10 8 6 4 2

BBC Books, an imprint of Ebury Publishing
20 Vauxhall Bridge Road,
London SW1V 2SA

BBC Books is part of the Penguin Random House group of companies
whose addresses can be found at global.penguinrandomhouse.com

Penguin
Random House
UK

Dismemberment © James Goss 2018
Lords and Masters © Cavan Scott 2018
Teddy Sparkles Must Die! © Paul Magrs 2018
The Liar, the Glitch and the War Zone © Peter Anghelides 2018
Girl Power! © Jacqueline Rayner 2018
Alit in Underland © Richard Dinnick 2018

James Goss, Cavan Scott, Paul Magrs, Peter Anghelides, Jacqueline Rayner and
Richard Dinnick have asserted their right to be identified as the authors of this
Work in accordance with the Copyright, Designs and Patents Act 1988

Doctor Who is a BBC Wales production
Executive producers: Steven Moffat and Brian Minchin

BBC, DOCTOR WHO and TARDIS (word marks, logos and devices) are
trademarks of the British Broadcasting Corporation and are used under licence.

First published by BBC Books in 2018

www.penguin.co.uk

A CIP catalogue record for this book is available from the British Library

ISBN 9781785943232

Editorial Director: Albert DePetrillo
Project Editor Steve Cole
Cover design: Lee Binding © Woodland Books Ltd, 2015

Typeset in India by Integra Software Services Pvt. Ltd, Pondicherry

Printed and bound in Great Britain by Clays Ltd, St Ives PLC

Penguin Random House is committed to a sustainable future for our
business, our readers and our planet. This book is made from Forest
Stewardship Council® certified paper.

MIX
Paper from
responsible sources
FSC® C018179
www.fsc.org

BBC

DOCTOR WHO

THE
MISSY
CHRONICLES

Contents

Dismemberment

James Goss

There is a tradition, and there is a chair to go with it.

The Scoundrels Club was one of London's oldest, most exclusive private members' clubs. The blasphemous bard Christopher Marlowe was a founder member, as were a whole host of spies, knaves and pirates – the very, very worst people that the British Empire had ever produced. All of them holding court in the club's marbled halls, scheming over the billiard tables, conniving over cigars, or simply dozing and dreaming of scandal in the club's wealth of leather chairs (some of the leather was fashioned from the hides of extinct species, or, in one case, an unwanted wife).

A particular seat had, for a considerable number of years, been the Master's home from home. He liked the light from the fire, the view it afforded of St James's Park, and it was right by the bell, which summoned a butler from behind a bookcase to attend to his every whim.

The Master had a tradition: whenever he changed body, he headed for the Scoundrels, he settled himself down in his chair, and he gathered his wits about him. Like most habits, he had no idea how he had acquired it, but it appealed to him. Plus, he knew that if the Doctor ever found out about it, it would annoy him no end. No matter how battered the Master was in spirit or body, he could sit here and remember former glories – the time he'd sat down for cigars with the Chinese Ambassador (shortly before having him devoured by dragons); the occasion he'd sold Lord Sutcliffe a giant whale over dinner; why, his copy of Magna Carta even hung in the map room (bringing back fond memories of his attempt to alter history with a singing robot).

The Master knew that he could stride in here, no matter how different he looked, and no one would raise an eyebrow. He would simply adopt his chair, summon a pot of something reviving, and peruse the paper, looking for the cartoons, or any really funny wars.

This time, however, there was a problem.

Harrison Mandeville was the Head of the Scoundrels' feared 1702 Committee. Nothing happened at the Scoundrels without his knowledge. He ran the place just how his members liked it – with the air of a miserable English public school. The heating went on every November 1st and came off on March 12th. The food was expensive but awful. The porters wore starched blazers. There was even a cricket team (which never played). Mandeville took a particular pleasure in blackballing African dictators' membership applications, though only after they'd bribed him handsomely. And if the bribes came from funds intended for hospitals, so much the better.

Mandeville occupied a secluded corner of the upper library where he could enjoy the view of traffic wardens at work. He was seldom disturbed, and that was how he liked it.

He let the butler stand before him for a full minute before he acknowledged him.

'Well? What is it?'

'Sir,' the butler stammered. 'The most terrible thing has happened.'

'Indeed?' Mandeville raised an eyebrow. He knew terrible. He'd once run a fashion show in North Korea.

'Sir. There's a … a *woman* in the members' lounge.'

Mandeville blanched. The Scoundrels had harboured many awful people over the years. Hawley Crippen had hidden out in its chambers before fleeing the authorities, Oswald Mosley had taken shelter from a mob, the bank robber Lytton had kept bullion in the cellar, but never, never, never before had the Scoundrels entertained a woman. Well, not a living one.

'She is sat in *his* chair – you know, second from the fire – and she has ordered afternoon tea.'

Mandeville stood, eyes blazing with the happy fury of a man who knew that he was completely in the right.

'Very well. Something must be done,' he announced, tugging at his whiskers. 'And I'm the man to do it.'

Mandeville sensed all eyes on him as he prowled across the lounge (the carpet had been torn from a mosque during the fall of Constantinople). Hands shook as they gripped newspapers. Ice cubes jingled angrily in tumblers. Throats were cleared menacingly. Every man expected Mandeville to do his duty.

Mandeville reached the Master's chair and stared, freshly aghast.

Not only was a woman sat in the chair, but she embodied absolutely all the worst aspects of his childhood – the flowing plum skirts of his nanny, the distant, cruel beauty of his mother. She was currently smearing strawberry jam on a slice of cucumber.

He cleared his throat.

She loaded a dollop of clotted cream on the cucumber, then looked up at him with a smile. Her eyes possessed that cold burn you got from holding ice. Her smile twitched this way and that, as though constantly changing its mind.

'Ye-es? Have you brought me more jam?'

'Jam?'

'Oh yes, I was begging for apricot.' She bit down on the slice of cucumber with a snap that echoed from the walls.

'I am not bringing you apricot jam.' Mandeville had, over the years, acquired a deadpan delivery which worked wonderfully when firing people.

'Then you can go.' The woman waved him away, picked up another slice of cucumber, applied some more jam to it, and this time nibbled at it with the delicacy of a piranha.

'The person who is going, madam, is you,' announced Mandeville, enjoying his moment.

'Me?' The cucumber was dropped into a cup of tea, where it floated uncertainly. 'I'm not going anywhere.' Her lips tugged themselves unwillingly towards a grin. 'And certainly not before I get some apricot jam.'

'This club,' Mandeville's voice bulldozered on, 'is for gentlemen only. Gentlemen who are elected. Gentlemen who are revered by their peers. It is not a watering hole for lady shoppers who wander in off the streets.'

The woman picked up a teaspoon and, with no effort at all, scored a noughts and crosses board into the marquetry of the table. 'I *am* a member. I have been a member since the Great Fire Of London.' A pause. She brightened, remembering something. 'I was the one who organised the fireworks party on the roof.' She flicked the teaspoon up and tapped it against her teeth. 'Look at me. You can see who I am. This is my chair. I've sat in it wearing several different bodies and once as a snake without a murmur. Don't be boring.'

'If what you say is true, you've just ruined a table and the club's reputation,' Mandeville coughed. 'Once a fellow is a member, he stays a member for life. We do not discriminate. We do not ask questions. But we *do* ask that he remains a *he*. The one thing that the Scoundrels Club has never been is fashionable.' He glowered at her. 'The door is over there. The waiters will be delighted to show you to it.'

The woman yawned, a yawn so deep that she could poke her vocal cords with the teaspoon. So she did. Then she stood up, and looked at the chairs around her.

'Oi, you lot,' she bellowed. The men in the chairs hid further behind their papers. 'You all know it's me. You do. I've just been through a traumatic experience. What I need is a sit down, a cuppa and to put my feet up – if not on a pile of dead bodies then a stool will do fine. The simple fact is I'm tired, and this place – in its own silly way – feels like home.'

The newspapers barely stirred in the breeze.

The woman put her hands on her hips. 'You lot – you're the closest things I have to friends. By which I mean you're awful, loathsome people – but you're *my* kind of people. Lord Ascot – remember when I helped you out with those naughty Swiss bankers by arranging that skiing trip for them on Everest? And Bobo – how many of your wives have I taken to the zoo … after dark? And what about you, Surgeon?' She kicked the chair nearest the fire which housed Harley Street's finest sawbones. 'Who do you come crying to whenever you need human test subjects? And don't I always deliver – kicking, screaming and quite free range?'

Her appeal met with unanimous silence. Even the Surgeon merely tutted.

'Listen to me. I need refuge, I need succour, most of all, I need a scone. What do you say? Guys? Lads? Boys?'

The Scoundrels Club had a grand entrance with polished brass and a polished doorman. It also had a door for trades, rubbish and laundry. Through this was flung the woman. She landed heavily on the pavement in a heap of crumpled cloth.

She looked back at Mandeville, flanked in the doorway by three of the burliest porters.

'So,' she said, holding up a broken umbrella. 'This is how you want to play it?'

Mandeville nodded. 'There is no place for you here.' He reached into a pocket and pulled out a jar. He tossed it at her. 'Your jam.'

It broke on the pavement. For a moment, he thought she was going to cry. Instead she dabbed at the mixture of jam and glass and licked her finger. 'Almost worth it,' she considered. She stood, brushing down her skirt.

Standing in front of the Scoundrels Club, she looked tired, she looked ill, and she looked crumpled. But her lips were curled and her teeth were bared. She raised a fist and shook it at the club.

'You may think I have the body of a weak and feeble woman. But I have a time machine and absolutely zero morals. Plus, I'm exceptionally spiteful.'

She curtsied, turned around and skipped off down the pavement. Mandeville snorted and went back inside.

Lord Ascot was not only a leading light at the Scoundrels Club, he was also a dynamo of the London art world. No one quite knew where his money came from, and it was rude to ask, but he'd paid for the Ascot Gallery, and for the Ascot Garden Bridge which spanned the Thames and led up to the gallery door. The gallery occupied a patch of the South Bank that had recently been quite nice council flats. Well, until that unexplained gas leak, which saw the tenants temporarily moved to Blackpool … only then the flats had been suddenly condemned, and approval had been rushed through for Lord Ascot's glass and steel gallery.

The Garden Bridge was his lordship's greatest gift to the nation (although, strangely, it was often closed to the public so it could be hired out at great expense to private functions). The whole complex ensured that, as far as the United Kingdom was concerned, Lord Ascot was a champion of the people.

After all, what greater sign was there of his good will and philanthropy than his making his entire collection available to the nation? Even if it wasn't free of charge, he was still a great man, and all his cultural largesse distracted from the secret deals with shady characters, and even the very curious rumours that most of the crates labelled 'Ascot Art' that were waved through Customs contained anything other than paintings.

Tonight was the grand opening of the Ascot Gallery, and the great and the good put aside their little qualms about the big man (after all, it was free to get in and there'd be free champagne), put on their finest clothes and trooped over the garden bridge to marvel at the gallery.

One or two guests glanced up at the sky. It looked like rain. It is oddly unpleasant to be on a bridge during the rain; the world feels flimsy.

Only one of the people on the bridge had thought to bring an umbrella. Like her dress and petticoat it was purple. She greeted everyone heading towards the Ascot Gallery with a cheery wave, and quite a few nodded back, wondering if they recognised her. Had she been on reality TV? Was she that woman who went round dodgy B&Bs? Whatever, she blew them all kisses, and a few blew them back.

Then the threatened rain made good on its promise.

At first the people pretended not to notice. They were loyal Londoners and had long ago learned to ignore rain. They simply pulled up their collars, tilted their chins and pressed on. London expects nothing less.

But then the screams started. At first little yelps that caused people to look around in confusion – where was the noise coming from, who was making it and would someone please shut them up? But then the screaming spread.

It was raining blood.

Not the cheery ketchup of horror movies, but a deep abattoir crimson that splashed across faces, stained white shirts and cream dresses, poured into eyes and gaping mouths, and caused a stampede across the bridge towards the doors of the gallery. Behind them, the puddles of blood dripped from the sides of the bridge.

The gallery was not yet open. At the stroke of 7, the doors were going to be thrown wide, heralded by a specially composed aria sung by the winner of *Britain's Got Talent*. Instead, the luckless chanteuse was first at the locked double doors, pounding against them and sobbing hysterically. Two hundred other people pressed up behind her, screaming for the doors to be opened and shouting at the press cameras to stop taking photos.

The press did not, of course, listen, and made sure to catch everything, including the moment that the doors were finally opened and the crowd fell in, scrambling over, biting and tearing at each other as they crawled into the gallery.

Had anyone had time to look they would have noticed that the bloody clouds were being eerily specific, raining down only on the bridge and the gallery. Even the press photographers were completely dry.

Once the guests were out of the way, one woman strode across the empty bridge, snug under her purple umbrella. She paused outside the gallery, admiring the scarlet rain dripping down the side of the building and the tattered mess of banners and abandoned shoes.

'That's what I call a red carpet,' she said.

Inside the lobby, the horrified guests stood, dripping, sobbing and queuing anxiously for the dryers in the bathrooms.

Lord Ascot stared at them in horror. He had enough problems – the caterers were using the wrong kind of salmon; his jacket pinched; and now he was being accused of some bizarre publicity stunt. However, he'd dealt with this kind of thing before. People could, he had long ago learned, always be shouted at, and if they couldn't be shouted at, they could still be bullied, and, failing that, they could be bought.

Waiters scampered around with flutes of wine. The singer made a brave attempt at that special aria, but her heart wasn't really in it, and when blood from her hair dripped into her wine glass, she gave up entirely.

Lord Ascot abandoned his speech, muttered a few impromptu remarks making it sound as though his guests were the victims of terrorism, insisted that 'London was stronger than that', glared at them all and then unlocked the door to the exhibition hall. That, he knew, would shut them up.

The graffiti taxidermist, Tanksy, had been lured out of retirement on his private Spanish island to curate a series of masterworks depicting Modern Urban Poverty. Guests were supposed to be greeted by 'Cerberus' – a three-headed dog made out of three pickled Rottweilers.

Only there was no trace of Tanksy's exhibition behind those doors. Instead the walls were covered with paintings. Old-fashioned, simple, beautiful paintings. Paintings showing smiling women, brave men, dead birds and fruit decaying in bowls. All the paintings were at least a hundred years old.

At first no one knew what to make of the paintings. Luckily, the art critic of a newspaper had turned up (there'd been a spare ticket and her editor hadn't found anyone famous to go).

The art critic pushed her way through the throng. A minute before, she'd been rather intimidated by all this celebrity. Now it was as though they'd all melted away. She stared up at the paintings – at beautiful boats sailing into sunsets; at noble Romans dying nobly; at shoemakers laughing; at vases of flowers – and she just couldn't believe it.

'The Reissmann Collection,' she started yelling, over and over.

Eventually, someone Googled it on their phone and gasped. Two minutes later, everyone in the entire room was an expert on the Reissmann Collection.

Back in the 1930s, hundreds of thousands of precious artworks were stolen by the Nazi Party from doomed Jewish families. After the Second World War, grieving relatives set about trying to recover them, but the process was long and difficult. Occasionally a petitioner would strike it lucky – perhaps they'd be having a meeting with a bureaucrat about a certain work of art and realise it was on the wall. Mostly, it was all very mysterious and murky.

For years, the Reissmann Collection had topped the list of mysterious murkiness. All that remained of a family with exquisitely good taste was a group of amazing paintings – believed to have vanished into a Swiss vault. The Swiss banks had professed themselves entirely innocent. By complete coincidence, Lord Ascot owned a Swiss bank. He'd once told a journalist that he'd love to help, but his bank had never had any Nazi clients, and, even if they had (which they did not), they'd now be long dead. Under the terms of their account, the contents of their private vaults would have been emptied, and he would have, naturally, returned the artworks to their rightful owners.

Only here was the entire Reissmann Collection, adorning the walls of the Ascot Gallery. Alongside framed photos of Lord Ascot posing with some of the more remarkable works of art. Here he was with a Goya, there with a Van Gogh, ah, and pretending to dance with a Michelangelo statue. In each picture, Lord Ascot was wearing SS uniform.

Five minutes later, the waiting photographers were treated to the sight of Lord Ascot running from his own gallery, out into the terrible red rain, rain that had soaked into the walls of his building and was now splashing around in scarlet puddles.

It was only the fear of that horrible rain that caused the furious mob behind him to draw back, watching the panting, pot-bellied man run onto his bridge.

Lord Ascot made it to the middle and then stopped, a stitch snatching at his heart. Catching his breath, he noticed the figure watching him from the other side. She was smiling under her umbrella.

If a spider could smile, it would have smiled that smile.

'You!' gasped Lord Ascot, recognising the woman from his club. 'You!'

The figure nodded. 'I promised I'd make you sorry.'

'You've ruined me.'

The figure shrugged, then checked her watch with elaborate boredom. 'Time I was off,' she said. 'Could I trouble you to say something nice?'

'What?'

'Oh, I don't know,' the woman tutted. 'Just a pleasantry. No?'

She turned and walked away into the rain.

No one quite got to the bottom of what happened next. Many people claimed that the stampede across the bridge had weakened it structurally. Some people came up with some elaborate theories.

What everyone could agree on was that the Ascot Bridge suddenly and dramatically collapsed, plunging Lord Ascot into the churning red waters of the Thames and burying him under the rubble. Even more remarkably, at that precise moment, it stopped raining, and a ghastly sun shone on a river stained the colour of cheap red wine.

That was the last that was ever heard of Lord Ascot.

Bobo Braithwaite woke up tied to some train tracks and wondered if it was another of his stag-dos. It would be just like the boys to pull a stunt like this.

'I really have to give up drinking,' Bobo sighed. 'And getting married.'

Mind you, he thought as he tried to scratch an itch on his nose, he was almost sure he'd know if another marriage was looming. For one thing there'd have been meetings with lawyers. Probably saying, 'Oh Bobo, not again.' Then again, his lawyers were always saying that.

Bobo was an entrepreneur – he built motorways, he ran trains, he jumped out of aeroplanes (he owned a fleet of them) – and, gosh, everyone loved Bobo. He wasn't conventional. He said outrageous things, all of them muttered through a mop of untidy hair. And if you wanted someone to launch your event, then he'd not only parachute in, he'd do it wearing a Union Jack nappy.

Even the people who hated Bobo still admired him in a way. He was a dynamo, a powerhouse. He created jobs, he made things happen, and everyone wanted a piece of him. He was being talked about as a possible transport minister. 'But gosh,' he'd said when asked about it. 'What can they want with me? Politicians are clever chaps, and I'm just a big mouth and I'm always popping my foot in it. No no no. I'd much rather get on with it and get the job done on time and without spending too much dosh.'

After that carefully calculated outburst, the cries to make him transport minister had only grown in intensity. Bobo didn't intend to take the job, of course, but the talk of it made sorting out contracts for his various ventures much more easy.

But why was he tied to a train track? Bobo gave up trying to scratch his nose and pondered his situation. The train track was not comfortable, but his surroundings were idyllic. What a lovely bit of unspoilt countryside to put a train line through. 'God's own country,' he thought.

Then he understood. *That* was why he was tied to a train track, of course! Silly Bobo!

'Publicity stunt,' he said, happily, and looked around for the cameras so he could give it his Best-of-British all.

Any minute now, why, yes, the director would appear, telling him how splendidly he was doing.

Classic Bobo. Doing an advert for his new high-speed train line strapped down to his own track.

Why, he could see a figure wandering towards him across a meadow. Now, if it had been a stag-do then she'd have made a very odd kissogram – dressed up in flowing plum skirts, poking at the daisies with her parasol. Mind you, she was probably the director of the advert. They let women do all sorts of things these days. And very splendidly they did them too.

The woman stopped, seemed to notice him for the first time, and acted with pantomime surprise at discovering him. Bobo laughed along.

'Hallooo there!' he called to her. 'How am I doing? Hope I'm not being too hopelessly dreadful.' Always good to come across as eager to please. People liked that.

'Oh no,' the woman replied. 'You're doing a simply lovely job ... of being a victim.' She hopped over a low fence and slid down the narrow embankment onto the line. As she did so she said, 'Wheeeeee.'

Bobo frowned and blew some hair out of his eyes. Crikey. This woman seemed familiar. Vague memory of her seeming to be quite angry and vowing revenge. Which, given Bobo's experience of the opposite sex, didn't really narrow it down that much.

No. Wait.

Gosh.

'I remember you,' he said, and, for the first time he felt a slight shiver in this perfect summer's day. 'From my club. The woman ... well ... the woman who wanted to be a member.'

'I am a member!' she said, exasperated. She angrily picked up a buttercup, and started to coo, 'He loves me, he loves me not' as she pulled at the petals.

'Oh, well done you!' Bobo wriggled against the rope tying him down. 'You don't need a stuffy old club. Why, look at you – directing this advert. I say. It is an advert, isn't it?'

The woman dropped the beheaded flower and leaned over him, confidential. 'Little secret. It's not an advert.'

'Oh.'

The woman did an impression of a steam train, including pistoning her elbows.

'Why are you doing that?'

'Chuff chuff chuff. Doing what? Chuff chuff chuff.'

'Pretending to be a steam train.'

'Because you like trains, Bobo dear. Poot, poot.' She stood up, surveying the track. 'And what a train line this is! High speed. Whoosh. Going through some quite dolly fields at vast public expense and a staggering amount of corruption.' She winked, slyly. 'That's between you and me. But I've read the accounts.' She yawned. 'What a lot of naughty numbers.'

Bobo harrumphed. That was just how one did business. Something showy and public and very exciting. Oodles of profit for yours truly and no promises broken because one never quite made any.

'Forgive me if I'm being a dense duffer, but why am I tied to this train track?'

The woman laughed. 'It's because I'm going to marry you.'

Ah, thought Bobo, miserably. It had been a stag-do after all. And he really was getting married again. He looked at the woman, uncertainly. Crumbs. 'I'm sorry, I don't recall—'

'You want to get off this train track don't you?' The woman rapped the rails with her umbrella. The line sang. 'I mean, there could be a train heading towards you at any moment. I imagine you'd hear it. Shoof-ta-kuff, shoof-ta-kuff. Wooo Wooo. Most exciting. Well, until it runs you over.'

Bobo considered his options. He'd married worse. 'All right, I'll say "*I do*".'

'You *do*? Oh lovely. You've made me the happiest woman alive.' The woman did a little dance, then stuck two fingers in her mouth and made a shrill whistle. 'Reverend! You're on!'

Footsteps crunched hurriedly along the gravel and a throat was cleared in a uniquely professional way. Bobo wasn't surprised to see a vicar trot into view.

'We're getting married here? Now?' said Bobo.

'Why not?' declared the woman. 'I'm impulsive. You're impulsive. And I brought a cake.' She took her hat off and looked inside it and then frowned. 'Well. Maybe I ate the cake. Anyway.' She clapped her fingers together and the vicar opened his prayer book.

The woman put her hand confidentially to the side of her mouth. 'This is the Reverend St John Colquhoun.'

'I, ah, used to be the pastor of the parish of St Mede's,' the vicar essayed in a plummy wobble. 'Lovely spot.'

'I must visit,' Bobo offered politely.

'Oh, you are visiting,' the vicar said dryly. 'The church used to be right here. Before you had it bulldozed to make way for your train line.'

'He's very cross with you,' the woman confided in a stage whisper.

'Oh gosh,' sighed Bobo dolorously. 'Gosh and golly.' This tactic had got him out of several scrapes in the past. 'As Petronius wrote in *The Satyricon*—'

The woman snapped her fingers. 'No time for that.' She tipped her head to one side. 'Ding-dong, the bells are going to chime.' She turned to the Rev Colquhoun. 'GET ME MARRIED,' she screamed.

So the vicar did, with a steely indifference to the groom being tied to a train line. When he reached the part that ponders 'If any of you know cause or just impediment why these persons should not be joined together in Holy Matrimony, ye are to declare it,' he magnificently ignored the woman who was jumping up and down and waving her hands in the air and yelling, 'Me! Me! Me! Pick me, sir!'

The vicar cleared his throat, and cantered to the end of the service. He inclined towards Bobo with a dry smile. 'You may now kiss the—'

He didn't get to say 'bride' as the woman had already thrown herself on top of Bobo, smearing his cheeks with a thousand lipstick pecks.

'Done, my love, done!' she cried, laughing. She rolled off him, lying beside him on the track. She was looking up at the sky calling out the shapes of clouds.

'That looks like a moo-cow, that looks like a baa-lamb, and that looks like a subdural hematoma.'

'A what?'

'Funny thing about high-speed trains – they're supposed to run in a straight line. It's what makes them high speed.' The woman yawned noisily. 'Trains! I'm boring my own teeth out of my mouth, but it's true. Straight line equals whoosh. And this train line goes in a lovely straight line from A to B ever so ever so fast. Apart from here, where it does a kinky little detour all the way around the Chancellor of the Exchequer's constituency. Funny that.' She stood up and dusted herself off. 'It goes right over some meadows, some fields full of squirrels and toads and poor St John's church. And that does cause a little problem which we'll get to in a moment.'

Bobo wriggled in his bonds. 'I say, Mrs B – now's the time to untie me. You did promise, after all.'

Bobo's wife raised an eyebrow. 'I think you'll find I made no promises – a trick I learned from you, hubby dearest. And now that I've married you, a little document I recently had notarised by your slightly depleted and traumatised team of lawyers says – in big, BIG capitals – that I have all your money. If I let you off that track I'd only have you following me around trying to tell me not to spend it all on taxidermy and candyfloss.'

'Gosh,' said Bobo a few times as it sank in. And then, like a third former who's found his tuck box scrumped, he burst out crying.

With his head against the rail, he heard a vague hum, a vibration.

His wife started sniffing the air. 'Shoof-ta-kuff, shoof-ta-kuff! My bridal train's on its way.' She grinned. 'As I was saying, that kink in the track you so kindly included means that the driver won't see you as he thunders round the corner. He'll have no time to slam on those lovely expensive brakes. Poot, and I say again, poot.'

Bobo continued to cry.

The terribly wealthy new Mrs Braithwaite strolled over to the Reverend St John Colquhoun and took him by the arm. 'I do believe that trains are finally about to become interesting, vicar. Shall we stay and watch?'

'I'd rather not, if it's all the same to you,' gulped the vicar guiltily.

'Very well.' Mrs Braithwaite took him by the arm. 'Then let's totter off. I can always peep back over my shoulder for the fun bit. When it gets all splatty.'

It was a fine summer's day and the richest woman in England and the vicar picked their way through the daisies up the bank. 'You know,' said Mrs Braithwaite, 'how do you fancy being Archbishop of Canterbury?'

'Me?'

'Yes. The present one's about to have a scuba-diving accident. Poor lamb can't swim. Utterly tragic.'

The Reverend Colquhoun burst out laughing. The two of them walked away through a meadow that was all that was pleasant about summer.

Behind them, Bobo Braithwaite screamed and screamed louder as one of his newest, fastest, and sharpest-wheeled trains whizzed along the line …

*

Saffron's hut was at the edge of the sugar plantation. It was, if you'd asked her, a little too near to the plantation. Often she could hear the screams. But sometimes, the wind was blowing in the other direction, and she could barely hear them at all.

Saffron had her hut, and most of all, she had her freedom. This was reasonably unusual for an African woman on a farm in the south of America in the 1700s. But there were ways.

Saffron had done what she'd had to in order to earn her freedom. She'd had six children and she'd handed them all over to the plantation owner. This had not been without qualms. Indeed, when the wind blew in the wrong direction, you could hear her sobbing.

Giving up her babies had been hard, but it had given her freedom and a tiny bit of property. And she was able to watch her children growing up. She cooked for them. Actually, she cooked for a lot of people (it was how she earned a living), but she cooked especially for her children. Most of them knew who she was, and smiled at her as she handed round the bowls. She treasured those smiles as she sat in the hut at night. They were what she lived for: the smiles and the hope that they'd be free some day.

'You're my kind of person,' said a voice.

Saffron looked up warily. She'd learned only ever to look up warily. The woman approaching had a thin, cruel look to her – not unusual among the plantation owner's women. Saffron had spent some time working in the big house on the Mandeville Plantation. It had not been pleasant. She'd had her hair pulled, hat pins jabbed into her arms, and tea and bedpans thrown at her. By contrast, the men seemed almost kindly. And one thing she was certain of: the Mandeville men weren't kind.

So, of course, Saffron eyed the newcomer carefully. The woman was dangerous, that much was certain.

The woman surprised her by bursting out laughing.

'Your food!' she said, gesturing at the cooking pot. 'I fully expected to have to make up something nice about it. But it's actually – oh, I can smell it – it's amazing.'

Saffron nodded her thanks.

'I would introduce myself,' said the woman, 'but I'm still working on the name. A couple of kinks in it. I'm usually referred to as the Master.'

'You're all masters here,' Saffron shrugged. 'Even the mistresses.'

'Ooh, nearly.' The woman laughed again. 'What a squalid little place in history this all is. I've a friend who loves humans. Loves you like pet ants under a magnifying glass on a cloudy day. Sometimes I think he can only love you by knowing when to look the other way. Oh, it's like he's married to you.'

Saffron waited, politely.

'Waaaaaait,' said the woman. 'You said "mistresses". And that's distracting me as much as that stew.'

'You want some stew?'

'It's quite taking my mind off what I was going to say. And I'm trying to plan here. Properly plan. Like with a capital P. *Mistress* ... Hmm ... Oh, so much going on in this head.' Pale eyes fixed on Saffron. 'I adore you.

I know everything you've had to do to get here. This little hut. Your little life. That heavenly stew. Come on.' She turned on her heels and marched away.

'Come where?' Saffron asked.

'With me. I'm offering you a job, silly. And bring the cook pot. I like morally compromised people but I *love* good cooking.'

One area where the Scoundrels Club of the twenty-first century *did* admit women was into the kitchens, and Saffron (out of her time but not her depth) rose swiftly up the ranks. No one cared that the Scoundrels' new head chef was strange and terrifying – all they noticed was that the club's food, for the first time in 300 years, was astounding.

When the Scoundrels' Annual Marlowe Banquet (thirteen courses and a reading of their treasured manuscript of *Dr Faustus II*) was announced, Harrison Mandeville made a special visit down to the kitchens to insist that the head chef cooked the feast personally.

'I'm busy.' Saffron was chopping carrots.

Mandeville leaned over the table and effected what was his most intimidating smile. 'But the club is counting on you ... my dear.'

Saffron shrugged. 'Fine.'

'Splendid!' This was just about the longest conversation Harrison Mandeville had ever had with a woman (including Mrs Mandeville) and he decided to leave it while he was ahead. 'You're a damn fine cook. As for your desserts! Dear lady, you really understand sugar.'

Away he went.

Saffron remained at her chopping board, dicing meat slowly.

The best thing about the Marlowe Banquet from Mandeville's point of view was that it allowed him to share his opinions with the other members. Thirteen courses may seem like a lot, but he ensured they flew by with topics such as 'What's Funny About Foreigners', 'There's Nothing Wrong With The Poor That A Good Holiday Wouldn't Sort Out', 'Why Tax Avoidance Is Good For The Economy' and so on. All in front of a roaring fire.

Seven courses down, he moved on to his own achievements.

Truthfully, it had been a difficult year for Mandeville. Harrison's (his chain of supermarkets) had had a few scandals – some dog meat had crept into the supply chain – and Mandeville took great pains both to explain his lack of involvement in this and also to argue that dog was, in many ways, a splendid meat. Having cleared that up (over a rather lovely rare fillet), he then amused himself with discussing the misfortunes of a few members. There was another of the Surgeon's malpractice suits, a few juicy divorces and the sad (but so discussable) suicide of one member's son.

Once he'd squeezed his fellows until the pips squeaked, he spoke about his pride and joy, his stable of racehorses. Senior managers in his supermarket had long ago accepted that they'd never be paid as much as one of his horses. 'Well, suck it up,' Mandeville was fond of telling them. 'If you put a foot wrong I'm not permitted to come after you with a shotgun. More's the pity.'

It might have been a tough year for Harrison's supermarkets, but it had been a splendid year for his racehorses. He waxed lyrical about the achievements of Downton, his prize stallion, hotly tipped to win the Grand National.

Once that was done, and a selection of delicious towering cakes and trifles had been accounted for, it was time to loosen one's waistbands and listen to the reading of *Dr Faustus II*, the lost play by Christopher Marlowe – a story so scandalous that, even though it was a short play (and lacking that bard's loftier turns of phrase), it was always heard in gaping silence.

Mandeville raised his hand and clicked his fingers for the manuscript to be brought forward. He opened the locked lead box, and looked inside.

Nothing.

The members gasped.

'What …' thundered Mandeville. 'What's happened to the manuscript?'

At that point the large fire crackled. A small scrap of paper drifted out of it. Drifted out of it, wandered through the air and wafted down in front of Mandeville.

The scrap of paper was the size of an envelope and crammed with some of the worst handwriting ever known to man. It was quite unmistakable.

Christopher Marlowe's.

Mandeville straightened slowly. He knew what must be happening. He was aware of – even mildly disconcerted by – the number of members who'd been dropping dead; he'd not forgotten the ex-member's threats of revenge. But he'd always imagined that the club was inviolable. It was, after all, a private members' club. Outrages did not happen inside. They simply did not.

He noticed the club librarian was sobbing: *Dr Faustus II* was their second most valuable manuscript. Well, let him sob! If that was the woman's idea of revenge, they could all weather that storm.

Mandeville performed that marvel of the upper-class man, the slow handclap.

'Oh very good,' he bellowed sarcastically. 'I'm a fox-hunting chap. We're not afraid of burning books.'

There was silence.

'Typical woman. Skulking in the shadows.'

That should have got a laugh. It did not.

Mandeville started to realise that the members around him were not just silent but had that peaky, mild sheen that normally came over a fellow after a glass too many of the club's brandy. 'What's the matter?' he asked, noticing for the first time that the fire was a little hot. He ran a finger under his collar – then realised it had stopped moving. Curious. The finger was just jammed there, in his shirt. How odd. He tried to stand, and realised that that wasn't happening either. He looked around the table and realised all the other members were similarly indisposed, their eyes rolling helplessly in their heads.

'Drugged ...' gasped the Surgeon to his right.

The doors crashed open, and the Scoundrels' head chef entered, followed by the club's most notorious ex-member. She curtsied to them all. 'So sorry I'm late. Just been running over a maths teacher with a milk float. You know how it is.' She nudged Saffron. 'Take a bow, my dear. MANDEVILLE! Saffron here – she used to be a slave on one of your family's dreary plantations. The ones you've forgotten about because it was so long ago and the money's still in your bank account. I let Saffron cook this meal for you lot as her revenge.'

'You poisoned us! You witch! You harpy!' Mandeville stood with difficulty, every limb shaking and burning with the effort. 'You poisoned the whole meal.'

The woman looked affronted. 'How dare you! That would have been an insult to the meat.' She stooped to lift something heavy from the floor behind her and heaved it onto the table.

To everyone else, it was just a horse's head, neatly severed. But Mandeville knew that noble brow, that clear eye and that tufted forelock only too well. Here was Downton, his prized stallion.

'My horse!'

'And your kingdom, yes, yes. Saffron here's cooked your whole stable. And you ate them all.' The woman stroked the horse's bloodied mane. 'No. Saffron couldn't have poisoned Dobbin here. That would have been rude. No, no, no. It was the *desserts* that she poisoned. After all, she and her family really know their sugar.'

The assembled members of the Scoundrels were starting to make choking, desperate noises. As the poison passed through its victims, it allowed them some movement – just enough to thrash around in agony.

The woman put her hands on her hips. 'Now, boys, I can't let you suffer. There is, of course, an antidote.'

Several pairs of desperate, popping eyes stared at her.

'Saffron!' she clapped her hands.

The cook, smirking with something approaching satisfaction, reached into an old carpet bag, and produced a book.

'Thank you, my dear.' The woman held aloft the book. 'Recognise this? It's your *first* most-precious manuscript. The only remaining copy of Shakespeare's *Love's Labour's Won*. Priceless and really rather dull, but Saffron soaked it in antidote.' She licked the corner of a page. 'Tastes very slightly of apricots. We all like apricots.'

She slammed the book down on the table. 'The recommended dose is about a page.'

The agonised Mandeville led the members in falling upon the manuscript, tearing the priceless pages to shreds, cramming them into their maws, chewing and gagging and swallowing, flailing as their limbs burned and spasmed. Punches were weakly thrown. Faces were slammed against the table. But, eventually, all the men took their medicine, falling back, gasping and croaking into their chairs.

Of the priceless, incredible manuscript, the only surviving example of Shakespeare's handwriting … nothing remained. Even the Surgeon was chewing grimly on a scrap of the cover.

'Will we live?' croaked Mandeville.

The woman just laughed.

'Damn you, woman, will we live? You told us we would live!'

The woman laughed some more, dabbing at the corners of her eyes with a lace handkerchief. 'Oh, bless you. Only stupid people trust what they're told.'

Mandeville closed his eyes as his fellow Scoundrels, gasping and groaning and swearing, twitched and fell unconscious.

It should be noted that the members of the Scoundrels Club didn't die right there and then. In fact, 'there and then' took on a whole new meaning, once they'd woken up and found themselves on the Mandeville sugar plantation in the eighteenth century. They were chained in manacles, trapped in a filthy hut with a lot of damp vermin sheltering from the storm outside. The recovering Scoundrels complained about this state of affairs very loudly.

Eventually, the door to the hut was thrown open and a large, angry man with a bullwhip strode in.

The Scoundrels demanded to know what was going on. They followed this up by further demands for warm baths, fresh towels, and a lack of rats.

The large angry man just laughed at them.

'Let me explain a few things to you, gents,' he said, spitting in their direction. 'This here is an highly lucer-ative sugar plantation. We're in the business of making the Mandeville family stinking filthy rich. Only problem is that yesterday I woke up to find my whole workforce gawn. Can you believe it? The whole lot scarpered. Why, when I get my hands on them, I'll hobble them all with a chisel, you see if I don't.' The large man momentarily lost himself as if in a rather gory reverie before finding his subject again. 'Anyway, that leaves me with no slaves and a lot of sugarcane to be harvested before these storms get worse. Filthy work it is, filthy. Anyway, there am I at my wits' end, when up pops a female pirate with you lot.'

'A female pirate?'

'Hey, it takes all sorts to make a world, that's what I say. She pops up with you lot – a bunch of bankrupts shipwrecked on the way to New South Wales.'

'What? How dare you!'

There was a short pause while the foreman kindly demonstrated to them how well his bullwhip worked. Once the whimpering had died down, he continued. 'I was only too happy to take you off your rescuer's hands for a song. And you're barely worth what I paid for you – don't look like you've done an honest day's work in your lives.'

This was, the foreman would have been pleased to learn, entirely true. He gestured to the open door, outside which the storm was raging.

'Anyway, can't sit around here gassing all night. The Mandevilles are not forgiving employers. So it's time for you to learn all about hard work ...'

Several hundred years later, Harrison Mandeville was running. He'd been running ever since he'd woken up. A voice called to him down the echoing corridors: 'Coooeeee! Cooooeeee!' He was being hunted.

Ragged, disoriented, his head buzzing with the after effects of being drugged, Mandeville staggered into the clubroom. There was a phone in there. There had to be a phone in there. And there it was, on the card table. He looked from left to right, decided to risk the open, and staggered towards it.

At which point a colossal dart shot into his left buttock.

Mandeville gasped in agony and toppled forward onto his front. Fire surged through his veins. A crossbow thudded onto the carpet beside him, and a voice spoke to him.

'Tut tut, you've fallen in the wrong place, you clumsy goose.'

Mandeville felt himself grabbed by the ankles and dragged towards the fire. It was roasting hot. He tried to flinch away. He couldn't move. And yet his legs and arms were being carefully, deliberately shifted.

'I'm just rearranging you. The first time I poisoned you, that was just a temporary paralysis so that you'd all shut up. The second time was knock-out drops. Now I've embalmed you. You'll make a lovely wee rug for ages and ages. And you'll be awake for all of them.'

Harrison Mandeville tried to scream, but nothing happened. He saw the woman, his tormentor, settle herself down in her chair (second from the fire, not too ostentatious), kick off her shoes and plonk her feet down on his skull.

'Finally! Oh dear me, this has all been exhausting, I tell you. I could die, all over again. But I won't.' She leaned forward, smiling with her very sharp teeth. 'Say something nice, dear.'

Mandeville tried to threaten her, but couldn't.

'Oh dear. Never mind. Forgot. You'll never be saying anything ever again.'

The woman settled back in her chair, easing into the soft leather and exhaling gloriously. 'All I wanted was a sit down. That's all. And you couldn't even give me that. And now look at what you've done. This whole club is mine now. I'm the last surviving member.'

From the chair nearest the fire there came a murmur of alarmed protest.

'Oh yes. I'll get to you in a moment, sweetheart.' She turned her attention back to her new rug, drumming her heels against it. 'I've picked a name. For myself. Lovely Saffron suggested it: Missy. Has a ring to it. Approachable. Gets things done. No messy. No fussy. Just Missy.'

The fire crackled.

'If you don't like it, speak now or forever hold your – oh sorry, that's tactless.'

The woman now known as Missy sprang to her feet and began to pace. 'What am I going to do with this place? Am I going to give it to Saffron? Turn it into a pound shop? Or just keep it as it is?'

Forgetting Mandeville entirely, she advanced on the chair closest to the fire.

Sat there, strapped into it, was the Scoundrels member nicknamed the Surgeon. He was staring at her in terror.

She tapped him on the knee. 'I know, this must all be terribly scary for you. All this death. It's morbid, isn't it? Mind you, you're a surgeon. You must have a strong stomach. Shall we whip it out and have a peek?'

The Surgeon gave a muffled shriek of fear.

'I'll tell you one thing I've learned about all this. Rich people – they're *such fun* to play with and so deliciously scared of dying. They'll do anything to avoid it, won't they?'

She nudged the Surgeon's chair a little closer to the fire. 'I've had a lovely idea,' she said. 'You're going to invent something. Something wonderful.' She kissed him on the nose and then stood back.

She started to rock the Surgeon's chair backwards and forwards, singing along to his muffled screams. One moment the chair tipped towards the fire, the next away, then in, then away. Closer and closer. The flames roared.

'Tell me, Dr Skarosa,' Missy addressed him by name now that she had one herself. Her smiling face glowed in the firelight. 'What are your feelings about cremation …?'

Lords and Masters
Cavan Scott

'Some people are *so* touchy.'

Parasol under her arm, Missy hitched up her skirts and ran through the stygian gloom of the Jesalorian jungle.

Behind her, the Skarasens roared. Three of them. Talk about an overreaction. Trees splintered like twigs as the monsters crashed after her, carving a path through the forest as they followed her scent.

Missy liked Skarasens. She'd even owned one once, a lovely little thing by the name of Flipper. She'd lost count of the number of unsuspecting allies she'd plunged into Flipper's tank over the centuries. How the console room had echoed to the sound of anguished screams and crunching bones.

Happy days.

Missy scrambled down a muddy slope, her parasol now gripped firmly in her hand. The descent was hardly dignified, but flair and panache could wait until she was safe. She didn't even have time to impale the three-eyed toad that watched her lazily from a nearby log. What a day!

A shallow lake lay ahead, the foul water bubbling with countless unknown dangers that roiled beneath its scum-covered surface. An island rose at the centre of the lagoon, home to a single, solitary tree. Its great trunk was twisted, smothered in greasy purple lichen, but Missy knew that no birds ever found shelter in its leafy branches, or insects crawled between the deep crags of its faintly vibrating bark.

This tree was different. This tree was home.

She did not look back as the Skarasens appeared at the brow of the incline behind her, nostrils flaring and eyes burning with bloodlust. Calmly, she unfurled her parasol above her head, the anti-gravity generators in the umbrella's ribs activating with the buzz of an angry wasp. Holding on to the handle, she rose into the air, floating across to the tree. Beneath her, fish leapt from the water, desperate to sink their fangs into her boots, as the Skarasens blundered down the slope behind, taking most of the soil with them. Soon they'd be in the water, but Missy would be gone long before they reached the island.

She drifted down to land beside the tree, her parasol closing as her feet touched the ground. Sensing her presence, doors opened where they had no place to be, splitting the tree in two. Light spilled out, illuminating Missy as she turned on her heels to blow a kiss to her monstrous pursuers before backing quickly into the opening.

The doors snapped shut around her.

Safe inside her TARDIS, Missy's heels clacked as she deposited her parasol in the umbrella stand beside the doors and marched towards the console that dominated the high-vaulted control room. Like the walls that surrounded her, the console was as black as a brigand's heart, its obsidian panels filled with a breathtaking array of switches and levers.

With a sigh, Missy leant against the console and closed her eyes for a second. This time she'd come so close. *So close.* If it wasn't for that pathetic cry-baby of a Zygon Queen, the Sizradian Hypersphere would have been where it belonged, in her hands.

Yes, Missy *had* double-crossed the suckered sovereign, and, yes, boiling the royal hatchlings in acid may have been inappropriate at a feast in the Queen's honour, but was that any reason for Brillana to set a pack of Skarasens on her trail?

The control room shuddered as the creatures threw themselves at the TARDIS, coiling their bodies around the counterfeit tree.

'Yes, yes, yes,' Missy said, as she carefully removed her hat and rested it on the console's telepathic circuits. 'I haven't forgotten about you lot. You can knock as much as you like, but you're not coming in …' Her hands danced across the controls as she spoke. 'Not by the hair of my chinny-chin-chin.'

Jabbing a large red button with an exquisitely manicured nail, Missy allowed herself a smile as the

Skarasens howled in pain. 'Sorry boys,' she said, 'but if you try to snack on a TARDIS, you'll get a mouthful of electrified plasmic shell.' Her stomach rumbled. The smell of charred flesh from outside made her mouth water. It had been years since she'd had barbecued Skarasen.

Poor old Flipper.

But now was not the time for a jaunt down memory lane, no matter how delicious the organic portions of her former pet had been. Missy had places to go and people to subjugate. The Hypersphere may have been lost, but there were other sources of unlimited cosmic power. Reaching into a jacket pocket, she pulled out a small leather-bound notebook, flipping through its yellowed pages until she found a list written in blood. Briefly, she wondered whose it was.

'The Cardium Heart? Too primitive. The Slarvian Astral-Core? Too volatile.' She stopped, tapping a finger against the penultimate entry. 'The Sun-Stealer of Tavos ... Now, that's a possibility, but the Tavosian Union will fight to the death to protect it. Do I *really* have time to commit genocide?' A grin spread across her face and she snapped the book shut. 'What am I talking about? I'll make time.'

Entering the coordinates for Tavos, she pulled at the dematerialisation lever, and ... nothing happened.

Missy stared at the controls in confusion. Where was the thunder of the TARDIS engines? Why weren't they moving?

She entered the sequence again, pumping the lever in frustration, but still the TARDIS didn't respond. She checked the fault locators. Everything was functioning as it should be: the helmic regulator, temporal accelerators; and the Eye of Harmony ...

The breath caught in her throat.

The Eye of Harmony, the energy source of this and every TARDIS, raged constantly with the power of a trapped sun. Now it was cold and lifeless, shut down remotely.

That could only mean one thing.

The thump of boots behind her gave the first indication that Missy wasn't alone in the control room. She turned slowly to find a staser pointing at her head. The woman who held it was one of her own kind; she looked young, maybe only 200, or 250 at the most. Her dark skin was smooth, her eyes almost black, blonde hair cropped short. She was taller than Missy, the body beneath the tight leather jacket and combat pants taut and lean, like an athlete. Or a hunter. Her grip on the gun looked equally strong, a golden band on her ring finger, her knuckles scarred from past fights.

The two women stared at each other, as still as Weeping Angels.

Missy wanted to rip her spine from her back, but knew she would be dead before the blood had soaked into the deck plates. *They* would see to that, from wherever *they* were watching.

The woman broke the silence at last. 'You're shorter than I expected.' Her eyes flicked down to Missy's boots. 'Explains the heels. Short Prydon syndrome. Seen it all before.'

Missy didn't move. She didn't frown or smile, but stood, hands clasped before her, as immobile as the TARDIS.

To her credit, the woman stood her ground. Her aim didn't waver, her hand didn't shake, although there was no mistaking the bead of sweat that blossomed on her brow to run down her cheek.

'Aren't you going to say something?'

Missy didn't respond.

The woman wetted her full lips. 'I heard you never shut up.'

Missy took a sharp breath through her nose, taking in the woman's scent. 'Arcalian,' she concluded, enjoying the muscle in the woman's eye that twitched in response. 'From the House of Stillhaven. Still in your first incarnation, but, ohhh …' Missy's own eyes lit up, glistening with interest. 'You suffer from Abridgement Syndrome.' She pulled a face, pushing out her bottom lip. 'No regenerations for you, poor baby. Still that'll make you easier to kill.'

The woman snorted, betraying her nerves. 'You really think that's going to happen?'

'Oh yes,' Missy said, brightly. 'You violate my TARDIS and point a gun at me. I've eviscerated people for forgetting to tie their shoelaces. Do you really think I'll let you live?'

A light flashed on the woman's ring. A communication signal. The trespasser's expression soured ever so slightly, but her voice remained professional and neutral when she spoke.

'Activate holo-link.'

A figure shimmered into being, a flickering hologram of a man wearing ceremonial armour and a haughty expression. His domed scalp was largely devoid of hair, his impressive nose held high and his grey eyes keen. It was a face Missy hadn't seen for a very long time.

'General,' she purred. 'What an unexpected pleasure. Would you like me to curtsey or bow?'

'I'd like you to shut up and listen for once,' the hologram replied, the clipped voice projected from Gallifrey, half an eternity away. Missy wondered if the General was standing in the Panopticon, or the War Room. No, definitely not the latter. She'd blown that up, hadn't she, before escaping Gomer's Asylum? It was so hard to remember sometimes.

'I assume this is your handiwork?' she commented, indicating the incapacitated console.

'The High Council has frozen your connection to the Eye of Harmony.'

'The High Council? Are they still around? I thought Rassilon ruled the roost these days.' The General's expression tightened at her mention of the Lord President. 'How is the old goat? Still choking on the White Point Stars I shoved down his throat? I hope his regeneration was nice and painful.'

'They say he screamed all the way through,' the woman told her. 'Ohila had to mix him a special draft.'

'Yayani,' warned the General, and Missy chuckled; not only had she learned the woman's name, she'd also heard the smirk in Yayani's voice as she'd described Rassilon's torment. Interesting.

The General's attention turned back to Missy. 'Control of your TARDIS will be returned in due course—'

'So long as I dance to whatever twisted tune Rassilon is playing this time. I know how this works. Been there, baldy, bought the T-shirt.'

The General ignored the jibe. 'We have a mission for you.'

'Then you've got the wrong renegade. Isn't goodie-goodie-two-shoes your usual puppet? What's the matter? Lost his number?' Missy snatched up the cross-time telephone from its cradle on the communication panel. 'Hang on, I have him on speed dial ...'

'The Doctor is ... unavailable.' The General raised his holographic arm, a globe appearing in front of his gauntleted hand. 'This is the Kyme Institute.'

Missy took a step nearer the image. There was a speck hovering above the planet's equator. She reached forward, prodding the dot with a finger. It expanded to show a space station shaped like a gigantic wheel.

Yayani's eyebrows shot up. 'Should she be able to do that?'

'No,' Missy said, rotating the holographic image on its axis, 'but I never let that stop me.' She glanced up at the General. 'So, why's this place got the High Council's knickers in a twist? Looks boooooooring to me. What is it? Twenty-seventh century?'

'Twenty-eighth,' the General confirmed. 'According to the Lord Prognosticator, a team of scientists are conducting a series of time experiments that may have catastrophic consequences for established history.'

'Sound like my kind of people.'

'Which is why we need them stopped.'

'And you can't be seen to interfere.'

'Gallifrey's existence must be kept secret. If our enemies were to discover that we'd survived the Time War …'

'The Universe would be ripped asunder, planets would bleed and stars would shatter.' Missy winked at Yayani. 'Just another Sunday morning for me …'

The General's eyes bore into her. 'Do you remember how I found you in the Siege of the Chronotide? Your screams for mercy as the Multiform closed in?'

For the first time since her TARDIS was boarded, anger contorted Missy's face into a mask of pure hatred. It was an expression that had struck fear into the hearts of supernovas and sent warlords and demigods running for their mothers, and yet the General regarded her with something approaching boredom.

'I'm not the Doctor,' Missy snarled, her nose millimetres from the hologram's imperious face. 'I can't be bullied or shamed. Those who try end up very dead. Try it again, and I'll rip out your hearts.'

The pompous idiot smiled, actually smiled. 'Without a TARDIS? I'd like to see you try. You can refuse our request, of course …'

'Then, I refuse.'

'… and spend the rest of your days marooned on this insignificant mud-ball.'

Missy looked down her nose at Yayani. 'Why not get your lapdog to shoot me?'

'And deny the Skarasens the thrill of the hunt?'

'Sorry to disappoint, but they've gone bye-byes, permanently.'

The General raised his eyebrows. 'Really?'

A deafening bellow rattled the control room doors, followed by another, and another.

Yayani had the decency to look surprised as the resurrected monsters renewed their attack, the walls of the TARDIS shaking beneath the onslaught. 'That's breaking the Laws of Time.'

'*They* make the rules, *they* break 'em.' Missy threw out her arms in surrender. 'Oh, what the hell. Let's do this. Perhaps a mission is just what I need to blow the cobwebs away.' She turned back to the console, sweeping up her hat which she secured with a long onyx pin. 'Give me the coordinates and I'll be off before you can say lickety-split.'

'No need,' the General told her, as the Eye of Harmony roared back into life, the dematerialisation circuit activating remotely.

With Missy's back to him, the General couldn't see her lips thin into a single line, before she forced herself to smile and wheeled around to face him.

'You really have thought of everything.' She snapped her heels together and delivered an extravagant salute. 'Orders delivered and understood, *sah*! Will do your dirty work like a good little soldier, and be back in time for kit inspection, *sah*, yes, *sah!*'

The General gave her a look that would wither Krynoids. 'Just get it done, and we'll release your TARDIS back to your control.'

'And never bother me again?' she asked, fluttering her eyelids, knowing exactly what the answer would be.

'Until next time, yes.'

Missy's hands curled into fists by her side, but she covered her frustration by planting them on her hips and turning to Yayani. 'And I suppose I'm stuck with you, too.'

Yayani nodded. 'I'm the High Council's insurance policy.'

Missy rolled her eyes. 'To ensure I carry out my mission like a good little girl.'

'Without any tricks,' the General confirmed.

Missy clasped a hand to her chest in mock outrage. 'Tricks? *Moi?* Perish the thought.'

'Think of her as your companion.'

'A companion who's ready to shoot me at a moment's notice?'

'Exactly.'

Missy's mouth twitched into a smile. 'The best kind. Well, don't let us girls keep you. I'm sure you have boots to polish and squares to bash.' She wiggled her fingers at the hologram in farewell. 'Bye-bye, baldy. Say hi to Rassipoos for me.'

Without another word, the hologram vanished. Missy turned, inspecting the instruments on the navigational panel. 'Are you going to point that thing at me all the time?' she asked, not looking up.

'Will I have to?' Yayani asked, expertly tracking Missy's movements with the staser.

'Probably, but if we're going to be pals, you might as well pop it away. I imagine you're quick on the draw. One false move, and I'm toast.'

'Flattery won't stop me from doing my duty,' Yayani told her, holstering her staser all the same. 'So, what next?'

Wiping a speck of non-existent dust from the console, Missy turned and walked towards the far wall. 'Next, we do what we're told.' She ran a finger around a circular locker set into the wall and it opened. Missy reached in, retrieving a leather cuff that she fastened around her wrist.

'A Vortex Manipulator?' Yayani frowned. 'Who in their right minds uses those any more?'

'Haven't you heard, silly? I've not been in my right mind since, well, forever.'

Snapping the roundel shut with a satisfying click, Missy strolled to the umbrella stand to choose a parasol from her extensive collection. 'Are you coming, or what?'

Behind Yayani, the central column fell still as they reached their destination. With one final resounding thud, the engines powered down and the eonic anchor deployed. They had landed. On cue, the doors slid open.

Missy's eyes sparkled as she stepped aside to allow Yayani to disembark. 'After you.'

'Don't you want to go first?'

'Why bring an expendable and get cut down in a hail of plasma bolts yourself?'

But there was no laser fire as they stepped out into a corridor; no running guards, not even an alarm. Slightly disappointed, Missy pulled the TARDIS door shut, savouring the tingle of chameleon shielding beneath her fingers. The time machine had disguised itself as a food dispenser, containing tasty snacks and treats for the institute's staff. Missy smiled in appreciation when she noticed that each of the brightly coloured packs was at least three decades past their use-by dates. 'Good girl,' she whispered, patting the glass window.

'It's quiet,' Yayani said, keeping her voice down.

'Oooh, do you think?' boomed Missy. She checked her Vortex Manipulator, Gallifreyan text swirling across its tiny display. 'The General has deposited us slap bang in the middle of the graveyard shift. Most of the boffins will be tucked up in bed, dreaming of particle accelerators. Pity.'

'Why?'

Missy gave her the look she usually reserved for simpletons and UNIT personnel. 'Because there'll be fewer to kill if they're all asleep.'

'Deaths are to be kept to a minimum,' Yayani told her.

'The General said that, did he? He actually said those words, in that order.'

Yayani nodded.

Missy blew air from her cheeks. 'Then, there's no point in me sticking around. You're on your own.'

She jabbed at the Vortex Manipulator, and then was forced to jab at it again when it stubbornly refused to operate.

Yayani crossed her arms and regarded Missy with infuriating amusement. 'Going somewhere?'

'Obviously not. The sneaky slaphead has fritzed this too, hasn't he?' Missy leaned in to Yayani conspiratorially. 'He hates it when people call him that, by the way.'

The ghost of a smile played on Yayani's lips. 'Duly noted.'

Missy cocked an eyebrow. Maybe there was something about this girl, after all. A light winked on the Manipulator's display, breaking the moment.

'Oh look, a map.' The Vortex Manipulator beeped and Missy looked up, peering down the corridor. 'We're on level six. The research facility is twelve storeys up.'

'And that's where we'll find the experiment?'

'You mean the General doesn't know?'

'That's why he's sent us.'

Missy rolled her eyes and strode over to a computer console set into the wall. Raising her parasol, she activated the screen with a blast of sonic energy from its tip.

'You have a sonic umbrella,' Yayani said, the scorn in her voice all too obvious.

'And I'll gut you like a gumblejack if you use that tone again,' Missy retorted, tapping the display. She fell silent for a moment, opening and closing information files at an alarming rate before she spoke again. 'I'm surprised they're still doing the tattoos.'

Beside her, Yayani shifted uncomfortably. 'Tattoos?'

Missy didn't look up. 'The Time Lords. Branding prisoners with biodata tags. Like the one on your wrist.'

The young woman's hand went to her forearm.

'So where did they put you? Shada? Capetrious?'

'They didn't put me anywhere.' Yayani nodded purposely at the screen. 'Well?'

Missy pouted. 'Awww, I thought we were going to share secrets and braid each other's hair and everything. Suit yourself.' She turned back to the terminal. 'This thing's useless, anyway. All the juicy data is locked behind a firewall. You need a biometric key.' She waved her fingers in the air. 'A handprint.'

'Well,' Yayani said, glancing down at Missy's parasol. 'Blitz it.'

Missy looked innocently at the umbrella. 'Blitz it? With this?'

Yayani gave her an exasperated look.

'Nah,' Missy concluded. 'Too easy.' Whirling around, she thrust the tip of the parasol into the air. There was a squeal of sonic interference followed by a klaxon that blared throughout the station.

'What did you do that for?' Yayani spluttered, drawing her staser.

'Because it's fun!' Missy shouted back, struggling to make herself heard over the alarm. 'Stand by for action!'

Armoured guards came running from every direction, pulse-rifles primed and ready to fire. Yayani cursed beneath her breath, her aim switching from one guard to another, until Missy reached over and slapped her hand down as if she was a naughty child.

'Oh, put that away, will you? We're hopelessly outgunned, and you know it.' She turned towards the armed men and shook her head as if they were in on the joke. 'You'll have to forgive my friend. She's new to the whole being caught red-handed thing. But don't worry, it's a fair cop.' Missy raised her gloved hands. 'We'll come quietly.'

'We will?' Yayani hissed.

'Drop your weapon,' snapped a gruff voice. A tall man with a fierce expression on his rugged feature took a step towards them. Unlike the other guards, he wasn't wearing a helmet, but the unwavering gun in his hand looked just as deadly as every other blaster pointing in their direction.

A compact laser deluxe too. A tasty bit of kit.

'I'd do as he says,' Missy told Yayani. 'I reckon he's the boss.' She peered at the name tag on the man's tunic. 'And I'm right. Chief Mitchell. Pleased to meet you, Chiefy.'

'You never stop talking, do you?' Yayani asked, bending to place her staser carefully on the floor.

'Not if I can help it. Now, kick it over to him.'

Yayani reluctantly obliged, Mitchell stopping the skidding gun with his foot. Satisfied, he took another step forward, his own laser outstretched.

'Identify yourself,' he growled.

'And what if we don't?' Missy asked.

'Then we shoot.'

'You could have done that already.'

'They want to know how we got on board,' Yayani realised.

Missy beamed at her. 'See? Not as stupid as you look.'

'I said, identify yourselves,' Mitchell repeated, his gun arm now fully extended.

'No, shan't,' Missy barked, slapping the computer terminal. Blast doors dropped from the ceiling to either side of them, slicing neatly through Mitchell's outstretched arm, rending his hand at the wrist. They could hear the chief screaming as the hand dropped to the floor, the laser deluxe still gripped in its twitching digits.

'What was *that*?' Yayani said as Missy scooped up the severed extremity with the tip of her brolly.

'I told you ... fun.' She prised the Chief's gun from the dead fingers and passed it to Yayani. 'Yes, we could have sonicked the information from the computer, but then I wouldn't have been able to do this.' Missy pressed Mitchell's rapidly cooling palm against the computer screen, unlocking the security system.

'Look,' she said, checking the logs. 'Research suite 1804 has chronometric screening.'

Yayani nodded slowly. 'So that must be where the time experiments are taking place.'

'You're welcome,' Missy said, slipping Mitchell's hand into a pocket in her skirts. 'To the eighteenth floor it is.'

To each side of them, the blast doors started to rise, before jolting to a halt, inches from the floor. Yayani pointed the laser deluxe at the gap.

'We'll have to get past the rest of the guards first.'

'Obviously.' Hooking her parasol over her arm, Missy tapped her Vortex Manipulator. 'Now let's see … General Slaphead has fused the temporal-shift actuator, but the teleport …'

She pressed a button. Missy and Yayani vanished in a blaze of light just as the guards finally forced open the blast doors and crowded through.

Twelve storeys up, Missy and Yayani materialised in a laboratory filled with gleaming equipment.

The sole occupant of the room – a pot-bellied alien with purple skin and numerous arms – swung round to face them in shock. He was wearing a white lab coat and held a datapad in his six-fingered hand.

'Who are you?' he squeaked as Missy tossed her parasol towards him.

'Here, catch.'

The scientist did as he was told, his fingers closing around the umbrella's shaft. Immediately, he froze, unable to move.

'Oops, sorry,' Missy apologised, pulling the datapad from his grasp. 'I forgot to mention the muscle-retention field that activates whenever someone else grabs my brolly. You won't be able to move until I prise it out of your useless fingers, but don't worry. You can still breathe, more or less.'

Missy strolled over to the door and used the datapad to reprogram the lock with a new passcode. 'That should keep security busy.'

'But will it keep them out?' Yayani asked, holstering the laser deluxe.

'Unless they can guess all thirty-two letters of my real name, I should think so,' Missy replied, smashing the datapad against a nearby table before walking back to the petrified scientist. 'Now, just what have you been up to, you naughty little beetroot?'

She scanned the contents of the work benches and computer screens.

'All pretty innocuous, not to mention *du-ull*. So dull, that I might have to knit myself a tea-cosy with your central nervous system just to alleviate the boredom.' Missy peered into the alien's troubled face. 'Unless, we can find the main event.'

Never taking her eyes from him, she licked the end of her finger before holding it up as if testing for wind.

'Ah, yes – time distortion. That's what we're looking for, Mr ...'

She glanced down at the scientist's name tag.

'... *Doctor* Kalub.' She gave the alien's cheek a sharp slap. 'The General *will* be pleased. He may even buy me an ice cream.' She brushed past Kalub, dancing up to a doorway at the far end of the laboratory. 'Do you like ice cream, Yayani?' she called back, swishing her skirts from left to right. 'Perhaps when this is all over I should take you to Rome, treat you to a choc ice.'

'I'll be heading straight back to Gallifrey,' Yayani told her, following close behind, 'same as always.'

'Well, we'll see about …'

Missy opened the door, stepping across the threshold only to stop in her tracks.

Yayani tried to peer past her. 'What is it?' Her mouth dropped open at the sight.

The creature was roughly humanoid. Trapped within a bubble of swirling energy, it writhed like it was drowning in water, its arms and legs kicking out into the air. No, more than that: the limbs were phasing in and out of existence, stretching back and forth through the lines of perception; solid one moment, like smoke the next. Its entire body was shifting, as were both its age and gender. It was old and it was young, a bone-white skeleton and a cluster of cells, man, woman, child, corpse, in constant flux and eternal agony.

Yayani swallowed, swaying on her feet, and Missy caught her arm to steady her. The younger woman grabbed Missy's hand, squeezing it, trying not to swoon.

'Chronographic containment field,' Missy said quietly. 'Don't worry, the dizziness will pass.'

'It's horrible,' Yayani said, trying to break Missy's grip. The renegade wouldn't let go, holding her tight.

'Why did they arrest you? The Time Lords. What did you do?'

Yayani looked surprised at the question. 'This isn't the time.'

'This is *exactly* the time.'

Yayani turned on her, her eyes flashing with anger. 'I tried to assassinate the Lord President. There, are you happy now?'

Missy turned back to the creature in the bubble. 'I assume you weren't successful.'

'What do you think?'

'But you're still with us,' Missy said. 'Still alive and kicking. Presidential assassins, even the rubbish ones, rarely escape the dispersal chamber. Trust me, I know.'

'They gave me a choice …'

Missy watched the creature twist and turn, becoming a swarm of particles before coalescing back into matter. She didn't speak. She didn't have to.

'I could be scattered across the Vortex,' Yayani went on, 'or serve the man I tried to kill.'

'On special missions. *Secret* missions. Hence the time ring. Pretty.'

Yayani snorted, playing with the band on her finger. 'Hardly. It's grafted to my body. A permanent reminder of my shame.'

'You could chop off your hand' Missy patted the bulge in her skirt pocket. 'Like poor old Chiefy.'

'And activate the explosive nanites they implanted into my hearts? No regenerations, remember.' Yayani swallowed. 'Turns out I'm a coward.'

'Survival isn't cowardice.' Missy took a step closer to the creature and reached out to touch its protective bubble, snatching her fingers back as the energy cocoon crackled and sparked. 'We're going to have to deactivate the containment field if we're going to put this thing out of its misery.' She turned to address Doctor Kalub, who was still standing motionless in the other room. 'How do you activate it? The interface?' She huffed when no answer came. 'Of course, you can't talk, can you? Never mind. I'll do it myself. I mean, I might hit the wrong button and blow up the entire station, but that's the risk we're going to have to take.'

She clicked her fingers and a cluster of holographic slabs appeared around her. She started working them like a concert pianist, cycling through Kalub's notes and methodology.

Yayani peered over her shoulder and frowned. The text on the virtual screens was indecipherable, a meaningless scrawl of random letters and symbols.

'Why isn't your TARDIS translating?'

'Because this isn't a language, not one stored in the TARDIS databanks anyway. It's an alphabet of Doctor Kalub's devising, complete gobbledegook to anyone but him.'

'Then, how are you reading it?'

'Because I'm exceptional in every way. Why did you try to kill Rassilon?'

Once again, the abrupt change in conversation put Yayani on the back foot, just as it was supposed to. A shadow passed over her face. 'I was alone.'

'No one to talk to and nothing to do, so you kill the Lord President of Gallifrey to pass the time? And you from the noble House of Stillhaven. What would your Patriarch say?'

'That's just it. I didn't have a patriarch. Stillhaven was silent, every hall empty.'

That made Missy pause. 'Every hall? Stillhaven is one of the largest families on Gallifrey.'

'Not any more. Not since the War. We voted against Rassilon on the Final Sanction.'

Missy's hearts skipped a beat. A memory flashed across her mind's eye, a memory from another time, another body. Rassilon standing victorious, staff in hand, flanked by two Time Lords, a man and the woman, forced to hide their faces in shame. She knew the woman of course, but the man she hadn't recognised until now – the Patriarch of Stillhaven.

'Rassilon used the rest of the House as test subjects in a series of experiments,' Yayani continued, her voice catching. 'Guinea pigs, isn't that what the humans say?'

'What kind of experiments?'

Yayani shrugged. 'I don't know. I didn't even know they were gone. He must have wiped my memories. If I hadn't found the recall cube that my brother used to play with as a child ...'

'You would never have remembered at all.' Missy's voice was softer than even she expected, as she shut down the bubble's safety relays one by one. 'I wonder why he left you behind?'

'I suppose he made a mistake.'

'Not in his nature.' From the corner of her eye, Missy followed the tear that ran down Yayani's cheek.

'Anyway. Doctor Kalub!' she called across the lab, as she reached the end of the scientist's notes. 'Still with us? You know, you're really quite clever. Genetically engineering a creature with a biological time-and-space-travel capability, and then imprisoning it in a stasis field. The creature tries to escape, emitting energies that are harvested as a perpetual source of power. Of course, it means never-ending pain for your poor little guinea pig.'

Beside her Yayani stiffened. Missy had chosen her words well.

'So, yes. Quite clever. But you're not perfect, not by a long shot. The dampeners are failing bit by bit. Before long, the creature will be free. That's what the Lord Prognosticator foresaw. It will escape, and the real magic will happen.'

She pointed at one of the holographic slabs, showing Yayani an X-ray of the creature.

Yayani leaned closer, eyebrows raising. 'It's pregnant.'

'Engineered that way,' Missy confirmed, 'so it has a reason to escape. It's not fighting for its own life, but that of its family.'

Mitchell's laser deluxe was back in Yayani's hand. She had turned, pointing it through the arch to the back of Kalub's head. This time the aim wasn't true. This time, Yayani was shaking, consumed by fury.

'Monster.'

'Just to be clear, she's talking about you, dear, not your creation.' Missy smiled as she finally managed to access the containment field's control matrix. 'I suspect she's going to kill you.' She broke off from the controls and sidled up to Yayani. 'Although a shot to the head? That's a swift death, almost merciful. Did you show this creature any mercy, doctor? Did you worry about its pain?'

Yayani didn't say a word. Her jaw was clenched, that muscle in the corner of her eye beating a fierce tempo.

Missy started playing with her Vortex Manipulator, sending commands from the tiny screen to the parasol in Kalub's hand. 'So, no shot to the head, that's out. I know! How about using the muscle-retention field? That *would* be nasty; and messy too, thinking about it. Every bone in your body cracked from within, your vital organs crushed into paste. Oooh, if it were down to me, I'd make it voice-activated…'

The Manipulator gave a beep.

'It's a good job I've just switched control to Yayani. She'd never put you through that all, even though you experimented on a living soul without care or conscience. She'd never contract the field, crushing you where you stood … and all by saying a single word…'

'What's the word?' Yayani asked, glowering at the helpless scientist.

Missy smiled, showing her teeth. 'The one thing we all fight for, in the end.'

She returned to the containment matrix, trying to lose herself in her work as the research suite lapsed into silence. She didn't even look up as Yayani barked a single word:

'Family.'

There was a faint buzz, followed by a strangled grunt and the delicious sound of bones popping, one after another. Missy didn't recognise Doctor Kalub's species and therefore had no way of knowing how many bones made up his skeleton, but she'd counted at least 200 separate fractures before the scientist collapsed into a heap of quivering jelly.

Yayani turned back to her, her face a blank mask. 'Are we done here?'

Missy acted as if nothing had just happened. 'Almost. You can see why Rassilon is worried. Natural time travellers running loose, multiplying like rabbits? Soon, the whole Vortex will be swarming with the things.'

'Why should the President care? There are plenty of time-shifters in the universe.'

'Like the Tharils?'

'Exactly.'

'Rassilon had them sterilised in the first year of the Time War.' Missy didn't look up; she didn't need to. She could imagine the look on Yayani's face. 'Then there were the Porfue and the Krajonnu ... No one can be allowed to threaten the Time Lords' supremacy. Not any more.'

'So, we have to kill it.' Yayani's words were a statement, not a question, devoid of emotion.

'Oh yes, that can't be helped. Poor darling. And that's the real reason they had to recruit me. The

Doctor wouldn't have the stomach for this, not with those bleeding hearts.' She finished, the holo-slabs switching off.

'What have you done?'

Missy picked fluff from her sleeve. 'The containment field is shutting down. I reckon we'll have at least three milliseconds before she disappears into the Vortex.'

Yayani held out the laser so she could take it.

Missy tutted. 'Oh, I think we can do better than that ...'

Retreating back to the door, Missy pulled the onyx hat pin from her hair. It was long and slender, ending in a bulbous black orb. Gripping the needle, Missy held it out in front of her, like a gun. The orb split into four, peeling back like the petals of a perverse metal flower, revealing another glowing sphere inside.

'What is that?'

Missy lips curled at the question. 'A TCE – Tissue Compression Eliminator. Haven't used one in donkey's years.'

'Then what are you waiting for?' Yayani urged her. 'Do it.'

Missy's expression hardened. 'Say something nice.'

The creature in the bubble howled, and the TCE fired.

In his chambers on Gallifrey, the General looked up from his desk at a familiar sound. He turned, looking to where Yayani usually materialised when returning from a mission.

His eyes narrowed. The girl wasn't in her customary place.

But surely that had been the sound of her time ring? It was unmistakable.

Putting down the data-scroll, he stood, walking over to the window. Where was she?

He stopped, spotting something at his feet. He looked down, and felt his stomach tighten.

A figure lay on the floor, no bigger than a doll. Its skin was dark, its hair blond. It wore a leather jacket, a perfectly crafted gun belt slung across its hips, and, glinting in the light of Gallifrey's suns, he could make out a band of gold on the ring finger of its right hand. The General swallowed, fully aware that if he examined the miniaturised body he would find a tattoo on its … on *her* wrist. A bisected cross, containing the biodata of one of his best agents.

He took a step back, noticing for the first time a scrap of paper beneath the figure. His armour creaked as he crouched down, carefully pulling the note free. He stayed there, on his haunches as he turned the paper over.

The handwriting was familiar, and the message clear. Three words, written in fresh green ink:

Not your puppet.

Missy's TARDIS slipped through the Vortex, heading to who knew where. The leather-bound notebook lay on the floor at the foot of the console, discarded, the list of power sources within no longer required.

Missy stood at the controls, checking the power readout.

Jettisoning the Eye of Harmony, that had been tricky, but not as problematic as trapping its replacement. She looked up to the scanner, watching Kalub's creature writhe in its new containment field, one that would never fracture, nor fail. Not that the creature would ever stop trying to escape. Missy was counting on that. It would rant and rail and scream and struggle, providing more than enough energy to fuel a Type 45 TARDIS. She was no longer dependent on Gallifrey, or the black hole trapped deep beneath the Panopticon. Best of all, there was nothing the General, the High Council, or even Rassilon could do about it. To think, she'd wasted all that energy tracking down a replacement for the Eye, knowing all too well that it was only a matter of time before the High Council came a-calling ... and then Rassilon had dropped the solution straight into her lap.

She thought of Yayani, of the look on her face when the TCE beam had struck. Poor, stupid Yayani. As if she'd found that recall cube by accident, or that Rassilon had simply forgotten she'd existed when he dissolved the House of Stillhaven. He thought he'd got what he'd wanted, yet again.

Not this time.

Missy walked over to the locker in the wall, depositing her Vortex Manipulator through the open door, before pulling a compact laser deluxe from her pocket and placing it beside the leather cuff.

She was truly free, for the first time in years, and she wasn't the only one.

'You're welcome, dear,' Missy said aloud, her fingers lingering on the laser gun before she sealed the roundel and strode from the control room.

Teddy Sparkles Must Die!
Paul Magrs

'Oh, do hurry, Jack. We shouldn't even be here. Look, she'll be back soon, and if she finds us in her room, I'm sure she'll be absolutely furious with us ...'

Jack spared his younger sister a scornful glance. 'I'm not scared of her. She's only a servant.'

Esme was 8, and she thought her older brother was the bravest person in the world, but breaking into the new governess's bedroom seemed more foolhardy than anything else. 'Please, Jack. Let's just go. Look, Peter's getting frightened.'

Their brother, who was only 5, was looking about the dimly lit bedroom with great interest. 'Boop,' he said. For some reason it was the only word he ever said.

'Look,' said Jack, peering under the tidily made bed. 'We agreed, didn't we? This new governess needs investigating. There's clearly something fishy about her, and none of the grown-ups will listen to a word we say.'

'Father thinks she's wonderful. Even Mrs Monk says she's a boon to the household.'

'But we know there's something decidedly queer going on, don't we?'

'I suppose so …'

'And we need to get to the bottom of it, don't we?'

'Boop,' said Peter.

'See? Peter agrees with me. Now, stand back. I'm going to open her wardrobe.'

'Oh, Jack … do you think that's wise? We can't go poking around in all her things …'

'I think we must!' said Jack, trying to sound more determined than he secretly felt. Before he could change his mind, he threw open both doors of the vast, dark, Victorian wardrobe.

And that's when the children came face to face with Teddy Sparkles for the first time.

'Hello, there!' boomed Teddy. 'Who are you?'

It had all begun several weeks ago, with the mysterious disappearance of the children's former governess, Miss Pratt. There were some dark mutterings from the servants that she had taken off with a greengrocer called Bernard and it was all a great scandal, but something about the matter made the children feel rather suspicious.

'Miss Pratt was devoted to us,' Jack mused. 'She simply wouldn't go running off with a grocer. At least, not without saying goodbye to us first.'

Peter agreed tearfully: 'Boop.'

'But whatever could have happened?' Esme asked.

'Our new governess appeared on our doorstep the very same day that Miss Pratt vanished without a trace,' Jack whispered. 'Doesn't that seem a bit convenient to you?'

Esme's eyes widened in shock. 'Do you really think she might have done something to … get rid of Miss Pratt?'

Jack nodded with great solemnity. 'I believe that Missy is capable of absolutely anything.'

'Ha! You're quite right there!' bellowed Teddy Sparkles. 'She's completely ruthless!'

The three children tried to shush him, but the small, golden bear couldn't seem to control his volume at all.

'But Teddy Sparkles,' said Esme. 'Aren't you Missy's best friend and confidante? Why, we listened at her door, very late each night for the past week, and we have heard you talking to her. We couldn't make out exactly what you were discussing, but you sounded ever so thick with each other.'

'She's no friend of mine, that awful woman!' Teddy shrieked. 'Crikey, no!'

Jack frowned at the bear's intemperate tone. The new governess might be under suspicion, but she was still a lady, after all. 'See here, Teddy – um – Sparkles. How is it that you're alive anyway? How on earth are you able to hold a conversation with us?'

'Aha,' cried Teddy Sparkles, jumping up from the floor of the wardrobe and executing a rather showy pirouette. 'I wondered when you'd ask!' He tightened his golden cravat and his topaz eyes glimmered with joy. 'I'm not any ordinary little bear. Oh, no, not I! I'm Teddy Sparkles! I'm magical, I am.'

'I see,' said Jack.

'Boop!' said Peter.

'Magical?' gasped Esme.

'I can grant wishes,' said Teddy Sparkles, trying to hurry them up. 'You know the kind of thing. We can go on lots of lovely magical adventures together. You can ask for anything you like and it'll all be marvellous, you'll see.'

'Goodness!' said Esme.

'But you must do something for me in return,' said the small bear.

'What's that?' asked Jack, narrowing his eyes.

The next morning, bright and early, the three children were at their desks in the schoolroom.

The door flew open and Missy came in like a waltzing panther, completely ignoring her charges and going straight to the tall windows that looked down onto the park.

'I do love the spring. Oh, look. A little bird. What kind of a bird is that, children?'

The children moved closer as Missy threw open the sash window.

Jack began, 'I think it's a—'

'Dead bird!' Green lightning burst from Missy's cameo brooch and sizzled the songbird on the spot. One second it was sitting on a branch singing a gay little tune, the next it was a shower of ashes. 'It doesn't matter,' Missy sighed. 'I hate birds. Nasty, squeaking things. Like children, really. I hate children as well, did I warn you about that?'

Esme shrank back, clutching hold of Peter as the new governess rounded on them.

'Boop,' said Peter, with some consternation.

'I especially hate nasty, sneaky, awful children who go creeping about in the boudoirs of lovely ladies behind their backs.'

Esme bit the inside of her cheeks hard to prevent herself squealing with terror. She stared at the killer cameo brooch on the high neck of Missy's sprigged cotton frock. She could frazzle them all to death in an instant: Esme didn't doubt it.

'You don't scare us,' said Jack. 'You're a monster. My father will hear all about you and the way you behave. We know what you've done.'

'Oh, yes?' Missy turned away abruptly, picked up a piece of chalk, and proceeded to write a whole series of unimaginably rude words on the board.

'My father will dismiss you from our household. You aren't fit to look after children.'

Missy turned back and snarled. 'I'm ten times the woman your previous governess is. Twenty times! A hundred times!'

Jack gasped. 'That isn't true!'

'Oh?' Missy stuck out her tongue and crossed the room to the cupboard where supplies of exercise books and pencils were usually kept. 'Look here, then.'

Missy lifted out a wooden box and opened its lid. The children gasped. Miss Pratt was lying crumpled inside, a mere ten inches tall and quite dead.

'See?' Missy sighed. 'She's neither use nor ornament now, is she? The silly, stubborn woman. You should be glad you've now got a teacher who can show you things your precious Miss Pratt could never even dream of. A teacher who can unveil all the secrets of the universe to you. Look, I'll pop her back in the box, shall I? And then you can go back to your desks ... and perhaps then you'd like to explain to me ... *just what on earth you've done with Teddy Sparkles ...?*'

'She is an utterly wicked and nasty person, and for several awful months I was her prisoner,' said Teddy Sparkles dolefully. 'Even with my amazing magical powers I was helpless. She took me away from my family and friends, and I fear I shall never see my wonderful home ever again!'

'Oh, dear, I'm frightfully sorry to hear that, Teddy Sparkles!' said Esme. 'But please stop crying so loudly, do!'

The children were crouched behind a jagged lip of grey rock and they were in the midst of a terrifying adventure. It was quite dark and they were each wearing rather cumbersome outfits with glass helmets.

Jack nudged his sister crossly. 'Can't you make that bear be quiet? He's going to get us killed.'

'Boop!' added Peter.

Esme took hold of the small bear and tried to hug him, but he wriggled as he wailed and soon he floated free of her grasp.

'Oh no!' she yelled. 'Teddy Sparkles!'

'Oooooh!' came the cries of the small, yellow bear as he drifted above their heads into the starry night sky. 'I really don't like zero gravity at all. It feels horrid!'

Jack pulled a face at Esme. 'This is your fault,' he said snappishly. 'It was your idea to wish for an adventure on the Moon.'

Now Esme felt like bursting into tears. 'I thought it would be exciting.'

'I'm sure it will be terribly exciting,' hissed her brother, 'when those Moon Men spy Teddy Sparkles floating above their heads, as they are bound to do at any moment …'

Just then there was a great hullaballoo down in the dusty crater because the Moon Men had, right at that very moment, spotted the bear turning cartwheels above their heads and heard his shouting: 'Oooooh! I say …!'

'Boop,' said Peter.

'Oh, this is an awful magical adventure,' said Esme. 'I wish I'd never suggested we learned the secrets of the Moon Men. They look absolutely horrible with their shaggy green fur and their eyes out on stalks like that. I hope we won't have to meet them.'

'I believe we have no choice,' gasped Jack. 'Look! They've noticed us standing here at the craggy lip of the crater! We're rather conspicuous in these copper-and-bronze space outfits that Teddy Sparkles magicked up for us.'

'Oh no! I do believe those hideous Moon Men are coming over here towards us with their savage-looking weapons!' Esme clutched her brother, and he put a consoling arm about her. 'Oh, dash it all. We need Teddy Sparkles to use his magic to take us home again!'

But right at that particular moment, Teddy Sparkles was no use to them at all. He was still turning over and over through the airless void. His frightened, booming cries had subsided now as he started to enjoy himself. 'Oho!' he bellowed. 'It's actually a pleasant sensation, this! Look at me!'

Jack frowned inside his magic space helmet. 'We're rather busy, Teddy Sparkles. We're about to be rudely attacked by vicious Moon Men.'

Esme squeezed her eyes shut. They were doubtless to die horrible deaths on the Moon, and no one would ever learn what had become of them. She wished her hardest and fiercest for salvation …

And help came their way, right at that very moment.

'Boop!' shouted Peter.

'MISSY!' Jack cried delightedly.

Esme opened her eyes to see their new governess arriving on the Moon.

'Good morning, you horrible, vile, detestable children. And who exactly gave you permission to go gallivanting about on the Moon today?'

She was drifting down from the stars with her sturdy umbrella unfurled. She floated as if gravity and airlessness had no meaning to her whatsoever. She looked mildly irked by the danger her charges had got themselves into, but hardly surprised at all.

The Moon Men came thundering up the side of the crater, waving their axes and scimitars about. They roared bloodthirstily and Missy sighed.

'Awful people,' she said, and then eradicated them on the spot with her deadly lipstick.

The children stared dumbstruck at the empty patch of airless void where the Moon Men had been.

'Now,' said Missy. 'What have I told you children about sneaking off on silly, hare-brained jaunts with that naughty Teddy Sparkles, hmm? One of these days that tiny, stuffing-filled fool is going to get you all killed, and then what am I going to tell your father and Mrs Monk the Housekeeper?'

Jack and his sister hung their heads. 'We don't know, Missy.'

'Boop,' added Peter.

'Well, I hope you've all had a dreadful scare and that it's made you see sense at last. This is all your own fault for stealing Teddy Sparkles from my wardrobe and giving in to his ridiculous suggestions for adventures you can share together.'

'But we like adventures!' cried Jack. 'Even scary ones with Moon Men ...'

Missy sighed. 'That's exactly what you said when Teddy Sparkles granted your wish to visit the Centre of the Earth last Tuesday. And just look what happened there!'

Esme shuddered. It had been absolutely terrifying, what with the savage, flesh-eating lizard people and the exploding volcanoes and all. If it hadn't been for Missy arriving just in the nick of time aboard that amazing giant Robotic Badger, they'd have been goners for sure.

'And what thanks do I get?' said Missy, pretending to weep. 'Insubordinate children. Inattentive children. Impolite children.'

'We're very sorry, Missy,' said Jack. 'We're sorry for sloping off to have magical adventures at the Earth's Core and on the Moon.'

'Also Mars,' she snapped. 'You made me travel all the way to Mars as well, didn't you? Just to rescue you from the palace of that ridiculous lobster king, or whatever he was. I had to wrestle a giant octopus in the royal arena, just to save your skins. It completely ruined my weekend, all that.' She looked down at her dark velvet coat and pulled a face. 'And now I'm covered in Moon Dust, too.'

'Boop,' said Peter sympathetically.

'Well, time to return home. Take my hand, Jack, and your sister's, and someone take hold of that horrid infant …'

'Wait!' said Esme. 'What about Teddy Sparkles?'

The bear was still spinning slowly above the Moon's surface, drifting further and further away. He was whooping madly, seemingly quite content to bob about in space for ever.

'I've a good mind to abandon that wretched creature where he is,' said Missy tightly. 'But I still have need of him. I hope you children have learned your lessons, after these jaunts of yours around the place. You must be very careful what you wish for, when it comes to Teddy Sparkles and his magical wishes.'

'We'll be much more careful in future,' Jack promised solemnly.

'Oh, I'm sure you will,' Missy smiled. 'In fact, I think it will be for the best if, for your next wishes, you do exactly as I bid …'

The children glanced at each other worriedly. There was something rather dark and frightening about their governess's tone of voice.

Just then, as she tightened her grip, came Teddy Sparkles' voice from the void: 'I say! I'm getting rather dizzy up here! Is it time for supper yet?'

Teddy Sparkles was looking crumpled and defeated. 'I've tried my level best!' he boomed. 'Those were fantastic adventures I sent the children on …'

Missy pulled a doubtful face, then went whirling about the schoolroom. 'I can't agree, I'm afraid. La, la, la.'

The children sat at their desks, feeling rather gloomy.

'Boop,' said Peter, disconsolate.

Outside there was September rain, drumming at the window and all over the Square outside, where the trees were turning orange and brown.

'The seasons are changing and it's time I was off,' said Missy. 'That's how it goes, I'm afraid, children. You have to make the best of me while you can.'

All three children were absolutely terrified of her, but there had been good points about her time with them, too. For example, the way she had rescued them after each of their trips with Teddy Sparkles had gone a bit wrong. Also, she read to them each night, and entertained them with the most wonderful stories about magical beasts in other lands. The books she read from were quite odd and certainly not available in any bookshops in London.

'We will miss you, Missy,' said Jack, somewhat stiffly.

'Will you, dearie?' she smiled and raised a quizzical brow. 'One day, you know, I might come back. One day when you least expect it.'

Some of the sparkle was returning to Teddy's golden fur at the news of her imminent departure. 'You're really going to leave us? So we can have fun in peace?'

She scowled at him. 'You …! Why, sometimes I wish I'd never kidnapped you from that silly little Planet of the Bears where I found you. You've been far too much bother.'

Teddy Sparkles looked almost pleased by this.

'But there is something you can do to make amends before I go,' said Missy airily. 'You can grant these children new wishes. Proper wishes. Sensible wishes.' She whirled about and glared at the children. 'And you three must wish for proper, sensible things, too.'

'But what?' frowned Esme.

Missy said: 'How about a bit of ambition, eh? What about wishing to become … ooh, I don't know

… let's see … the Head of the Secret Service, eh? Or Chair of NATO? Or perhaps … the CEO of Galactico Chemicals?'

Jack, Esme and Peter all stared at her.

'We don't know what those things are,' said Jack.

Missy rolled her eyes. 'Well, of course you don't. Not yet. But I'm thinking about the future and these are future things. They represent future security and success. You're very lucky to have me here to impart my future knowledge to you.'

'You're right, thank you, Missy,' said Esme. 'We'll take your advice and wish to become those very things. Whatever they are.'

'Jolly good,' said Missy, opening her carpet bag and throwing into it anything of value she could lay her hands on.

'Boop,' said Peter.

'Is this really a good idea?' hissed Jack. 'We don't know what any of those things are. NATO, and so on. It sounds all a bit queer.'

Teddy Sparkles coughed to draw attention to himself. He was glittering with magical energy, just as he always did, right before granting wishes.

'I bet that stupid alien bear can't even get the spell right anyway,' Missy sighed. 'His kind are supposed to manipulate the timelines and everything, but I bet he can't create the futures for you three that I've suggested …'

'Oh, but I can!' shouted Teddy Sparkles crossly. 'How dare you underestimate me, Missy! How dare you put me down! Look, here! I'm doing magic now! I'm granting those wishes RIGHT NOW!'

It was true, there was a very odd trembling in the air, rather as if invisible lines of force and influence stretching way into the future were activating and shimmering and obeying his mysterious will. Esme found herself growing rather frightened as the very air took on a golden hue.

Missy snapped her carpet bag shut and announced, 'Well, I'll be off, then. I'll see you all later. Much later, I hope.'

And with no more ado, she swept out of the schoolroom.

The children listened for her slamming out of the front door and marching out into the street. But instead she went back upstairs to her room, climbed inside her vast, Victorian wardrobe and shut the doors behind her. Then there was the most extraordinary noise, and after that silence fell in the attic of their house in Queen Square.

Missy had vanished from their lives.

'Good!' Teddy Sparkles bellowed. 'She's a dreadful woman!' Then a thought seemed to strike him. 'But if she's gone ... then I'll never get home! I'll never get back to Ursino Six! I'm stuck here ... in a world of human beings ...!'

The magic faded abruptly from the room, and the three children hurried to gather round the little bear in order to comfort him.

*

Several decades went by. War years. Terrible years for London.

Bombs were dropped by the enemy, even on the fancier districts. Great houses were destroyed as well as much humbler ones. Vast armies of children were sent out to the countryside, to new homes, far away from danger, it was hoped.

The children grew up.

The house in Queen Square still stood, and the family retained ownership, even as the children moved away, into their own lives. Their father grew old and fussy, looked after by his serving staff. He complained that no one ever came to visit him.

The children forgot. Life after the war was tough and complicated. They had careers to build. Families of their own to raise. Gradually they came to take up positions in the adult world. Important positions. Powerful positions.

And the strange events of that particular summer – when Jack was 10, Esme was 8, and Peter was 5 – faded away from their minds completely. Perhaps some lingering enchantment rinsed through their memories, reducing their adventures to mere echoes of stories told to them once upon a time by a peculiar stand-in governess who came, briefly, to stay.

The children grew into their thirties and then their forties. Their own children started growing up to question the world and the order of things. They came to visit their tetchy grandfather in Queen Square, and they loved the dusty, antiquated mausoleum where he lived. By the early 1960s hardly anyone lived in places like that. Houses such as his had been carved up into flats. The grandchildren themselves – four of them: Lucy, Dinah, Eric and John – all lived in modern, comfortable homes in the suburbs. But the cousins loved going to visit Queen Square whenever they could, especially at Christmas, when the ancient cook laid on a marvellous feast, and told them stories about the old days.

Christmas Eve 1962 saw all the children and grandchildren converge upon the old townhouse. It was snowing in London, and the whole day had been dark since lunchtime.

Eric – who was youngest and most fanciful of all the cousins – said it was the kind of day that magic might happen. The others scoffed at him, but Eric was sensitive. He was alert to things that everyone else in his family had seemingly forgotten.

It was Eric who was looking up into the drifting snow, on the pavement outside the house, and it was Eric who spied the woman falling out of the sky.

'The what?' John laughed, and called his cousins outside so they could all laugh at Eric's latest ridiculous notion.

'It's true!' yelled Eric. 'Just look! Look up there! It's a woman! With an umbrella! Dressed so old-fashioned in a duster coat and a little hat with flowers on ... Can't you see ...?'

She was drifting down through the snowy darkness to land on the pavement beside them. The children stared at her in wonder.

'Hello,' she said, lips prim and eyes piercing. 'I imagine your parents must have told you all about me?'

Missy asked that the whole family be gathered in the drawing room of the old house. Once they were all sat before her – some of the older ones wearing amazed expressions – she smiled broadly.

'Hello, again everyone. Don't I look magnificent? I haven't changed a bit, have I?'

Esme was aghast. 'You … You really haven't …!'

Her husband – a corpulent man called Alan – spluttered: 'Look, who the devil is this woman?' He glared round at his wife's family. 'What's the matter with you all?' They had always been a strange bunch. Rich and powerful, of course, but strange all the same.

'Not now, Alan.' Jack – who had become rather gruff and looked very like his father these days – decided to take charge. 'Look here, Missy. What is it you want with us? Tell us your business and then leave us in peace.'

The old man by the fire was struggling to concentrate on what was going on. He glowered at Missy. 'Isn't that one of the servants?'

Missy sighed happily. 'Now, don't rush to be rid of me again, children. I've come back to see how you are. You've all been terribly successful, haven't you? You've all done very well for yourselves, hmm? And you all know, don't you, that it's only down to one person …' She simpered. 'Me.'

Peter's wife was scared, clutching his arm. 'What's going on, Peter? Who is this person? What does she mean?'

Absentmindedly Missy took out her lipstick and adjusted the setting. She wondered about blasting one of the children's spouses into nothingness. Just for the thrill of it. Just to focus their attention a little. She pointed the deadly lipstick at Peter's wife and it hummed menacingly.

'Don't you dare vaporise anyone,' said Jack warningly.

'You do remember then,' said Missy. 'You remember your old governess and what she can do, don't you?'

All the blood had rushed out of Esme's face. Oh God, she thought. It wasn't just some childish game we used to play; Miss Pratt really had been shrunk to the size of a doll, and the adventures we shared, they … they were all real. She looked at the others and their children. We knew the whole time that we were deliberately not talking about Missy. We reaped the rewards and benefits of the things she made us wish for, all the while pretending that it was just a silly game.

But Missy was real, and now here she was, back again.

Esme took a step forward and made her voice level and brave and professional-sounding, as befitted the CEO of Galactico Chemicals. 'What do you want from us?'

'I think it's time for some payback,' said Missy crisply. 'And, to that end, what I'd like very much is if you combined all your power and influence, and arranged things nicely for me. What I'd really like is enough super-duper weapons and bombs and stuff like that in order to take over the entire world. All right?'

Everyone in the drawing room gazed at her as if she was bananas.

'That's right, I am,' she grinned. 'Bananas. And you're going to help me take over the entire world, aren't you?'

Up in the attic of the house in Queen Square, Teddy Sparkles was absolutely furious.

Though his powers were diminished he could hear every single word of what was being said downstairs. His magnificent alien brain had detected the arrival of the loathsome Missy as soon as she had manifested in this time zone. He knew she was back, and he knew why.

He would have warned the children and their own children, had he been in a better mood but, quite frankly, after three decades of being locked away in this drab and dusty place, he wasn't of a mind to help anyone at all.

His fur was lustreless, as were his topaz eyes. His golden sparkles could raise barely a shimmer these days. His toes had been nibbled by squirrels. He had almost given up the will to live.

He would never see Ursino Six again …

But still there was a fleck of hope in his heart. He still had powers. Not magical powers, although they were so amazingly advanced and beyond the ken of human beings that they might as well have been. Like other adepts on his home world, he had astonishing mental abilities that allowed him to see the warp and weft of reality. Like certain other Ursine mystics, he could refashion reality – both past and future – to his own liking. The children he had known here in Queen Square had believed he was granting wishes: it was their way of understanding the immense complexity of what he was actually doing when he cudgelled his brains and focused his will upon the workings of the multiverse ...

Teddy Sparkles began to shimmer and glow just then, as he remembered how wonderful his powers had been. Yes, he had altered reality and subsumed it to his mighty thoughts. And – if he tried his very best – he still could! He could make the very cosmos tremble ...

The door flew open and one of the children came bustling into the room. No longer a child, Esme was well into middle age now and looked very harassed. He knew at once that she had come searching for him, so he coughed loudly to draw her attention to where he was lying on the nightstand.

'Oh, Teddy Sparkles! The most dreadful thing has happened ...'

The bear did his best to sound reassuring. 'I know, Esme. I know.'

Her lined face was stained with tears as she clutched him to her bosom. '*How* could you know?'

Teddy Sparkles couldn't help glowing with pleasure at the sensation of being held and hugged once more. So many years! He had lain here so long, alone, neglected in this attic room that had once belonged to Missy and many servants before her. All through the Blitz and the years of Austerity. He had heard life crashing and booming and murmuring along below him, and everyone, it seemed, had forgotten Teddy Sparkles.

'Oh, Esme,' he said, becoming more emotional than he had meant to. 'How could you just forget about me? How could you leave me here?'

'I ... I don't know ... I'm so sorry ...'

'I fixed everything up, didn't I? I gave you everything you wished for ... You've all grown up to be exactly what you wanted to be ...'

Her expression darkened. 'Not really, Teddy. You see, Missy told us to wish for those things, didn't she? I never wanted to run a chemicals company. And the others ... they're doing jobs they hate too. Oh, we have power and influence, but none of us are happy. It's all Missy's doing.'

'Oh, dear,' said Teddy Sparkles. 'None of you are happy?'

Esme dissolved into tears. 'And now Missy is back ... and she's making the most ghastly demands of us ...'

'There, there,' said Teddy Sparkles, patting her heaving shoulders with his tiny paws. 'I will help you. I will do my level best to help ...'

'Ha!' There came a brutal snort of laughter from the doorway.

Teddy and Esme looked up to see Missy framed there in silhouette.

'Hello again, Teddy Sparkles,' she said. 'I've come back to take over the world. What do you think of that?' She peered more closely at the little bear. 'You do look a bit shabby, dearie. All the effort maintaining your timeline manipulations has taken its toll on your poor plush.' And then she cackled threateningly and stared at Esme. 'The world, please. Hand it over. And be snappy about it.'

The thing was, it was all entirely possible. Missy had thought it all through very cleverly, and it turned out to be all too straightforward for the children to give her what she wanted: the wherewithal and the means to take over the entire world.

'You could give me an island in the middle of the Baltic Sea, with a secret underground lair!' she cried, delightedly. 'And I'd have all the codes and things at my fingertips, for employing the world's various hideous super-duper weapons and setting them off, at deadly cross-purposes, all over the globe! With access to the resources of Galactico and the knowledge of the Secret Services, I'll be able to hold the whole world to ransom!'

At this, she began hooting with laughter, and everyone watched in dismay.

'We can't let you do this,' Jack said gruffly. 'You've used us, Missy. We can't allow you to take over the whole world …'

'Never!' gasped Peter. 'You'd do awful things with it. You'd make slaves of the whole human race ...'

'Yes, I would,' she agreed. 'Honestly, you've no idea how many times I've tried to do this over the years, and met with ignominious failure every time. But this time, that precious Teddy Sparkles has seen to it that my global success is inevitable!'

Everyone looked at Teddy, who hung his head in shame. 'I did try to warn you all how dreadful she is,' he sighed.

The children's father had completely lost his mind in terror. 'Boop,' he said.

'We're loyal to our country and our planet,' said Esme bravely. 'We'd all rather die than give in to your demands.'

'Oh, really?' smiled Missy.

'Let's not be rash, Esme, dear,' said Peter. 'Let's not get all noble and self-sacrificial before we have to ...'

'What do you mean?' she snapped.

'Well, perhaps Missy won't be quite as bad as you think she'll be. If she was the sole Mistress of the World, we wouldn't have any discord or Arms Race or nasty things like the Cuban Missile Crisis, would we?'

'Exactly!' Missy shrilled. 'Because you'd all be subsumed to my superior will!'

Esme gasped. 'Peter, I can't believe you're even considering the idea of helping her take over the world ...'

That was when Teddy Sparkles interceded. He was standing beside the children's father and he was glowing strangely, as if he had managed to gather together the last vestiges of his magic power. 'No one will take over anything!' he boomed, in his old, sonorous voice.

'Teddy ...?' gasped Jack.

Suddenly Missy looked furious. 'Don't you dare!' It was as if she recognised the nature of those waves of elemental power rippling through the air from the little bear's body. 'Don't!'

'What is he doing?' gasped Peter.

'Boop!' said their father, rocking in his chair.

Suddenly the atmosphere in the room turned quite strange. One moment it was simply the drawing room, with the decorated tree and the cards arranged on top of the blazing mantelpiece, with the whole family arrayed against the interloper. Then the room was swaying and spinning. It felt as if it was pulling itself free from the rest of reality ...

'Mum? Dad ...?' Eric stared wildly at the grown-ups. The other cousins were just as perplexed and horrified by what was going on. One moment all the adults had been shouting impossible things, and now this ... The room was bucking and rocking like it had been set afloat on a stormy sea. Eric struggled to the window and drew back the net curtains. The blizzard was coming down thickly now over Queen Square ... so thickly they could no longer see the park through the window ...

'It isn't there any more!' screamed his cousin, Alice. 'It isn't there!'

'We're going back!' boomed the voice of Teddy Sparkles, full of regret. 'Back and back and back through time …!'

It took a while, and it was a bumpy ride, but Teddy Sparkles managed to rewrite history.

He sent Missy spinning violently away from the Earth with a huge, desperate effort of will. Caught off-guard, she howled in outrage and swore further vengeance on his threadbare head.

Esme felt herself changing … She felt the nature of reality metamorphosing all around her, but above all she felt her own being unravelling. She found her own life reversing and unbecoming …

'Nooooo!' she yelled as she regained her distant youth.

All around her, her family members were doing the same. Her husband vanished in a puff of possibility: the same became of her brothers' wives. Most awful of all, their children simply popped out of existence, as if they had never been born.

Esme wailed in dismay. 'Noooo, Teddy Sparkles …! What have you done?'

'I am turning back time!' he bellowed, through the turbid chaos. 'I am using my incredible time-engineering talents to give you all another chance!'

Esme wept for her lost family and the life she had known. Perhaps she had hated being head of a global technological empire, and perhaps she felt her life had been unduly influenced by Missy, but she had loved her children, and her husband had been quite bearable.

'Do you mean ...' cried Jack, 'that we'll have to live our lives all over again?'

'You will get another chance!' Teddy shouted. 'Isn't that wonderful? No one else ever gets an opportunity like this ...!'

A furious lightning flash heralded the sudden return of Missy. Teddy Sparkles had managed to keep her at bay for seven crucial minutes, but now she was back in their midst, and snarling.

She spat and swore at Teddy Sparkles. She crossed the swaying room in three strides and picked him up in both taloned hands. 'I had world domination within my grasp, you horrid little brute!'

'It's done. You can't stop it, now, whatever you do to me.' He laughed feebly in her face; his time-engineering efforts had wrung him out. 'We are going back. You will be a servant again, Missy! And this time I will refuse to grant your wishes ...!'

His hollow laughter rang inside her head for the rest of the journey back to 1925.

Esme cried out in surprise as they arrived with a sudden bump.

It took a few moments for them to come to their senses. The children stared at each other in wonder.

'Look at you both,' Jack said hoarsely. 'Look at me ...'

Esme gasped. 'We've become children again.'

'All those years,' whispered Jack. 'The war and our careers and everything … All for nothing!'

Missy cast him an acidulous glance. 'I always thought careers were very silly things to have. Such a waste of time. Far better to invent breathtakingly ambitious evil schemes.'

'Except this one backfired, didn't it?' Esme shouted, jumping up, surprised at how much energy she now had. 'You've made an awful hash of this one!'

'Children?' called their father, standing up from his chair and looking younger, but utterly confused. 'What the devil's going on?'

'We're back home, father,' said Jack. 'Teddy Sparkles has brought us all back home again to Queen Square, in the right year. Everything is exactly as it was.'

'Hurrah!' shouted Teddy Sparkles, and Missy scowled at him.

'And all our lives in the future … almost forty years … were a complete waste of time,' sobbed Esme.

Missy shrugged. 'Most human lives are a waste of time. Trust me. I've met some awful, pointless, futile people on this planet. At least you lot get to have another go.' She sighed and picked up her brolly, and tilted her hat. 'I suppose I could brainwash you all into causing complete carnage with future Earth history by exploiting your knowledge of all that is to come … But I rather imagine that your future, adult memories are fading away as I speak, aren't they? Everything's withering and falling away like a peculiar dream, and so by now you've all turned back into a bunch of rather boring children again, haven't you? Yes, I can tell I'm quite right, as per usual. Ah well. I'll be off, then.'

'Wait!' yelled Jack, who was still staring out of the window. 'There's something wrong.'

'Well, of course there is,' sighed Missy. 'My wicked schemes have been spoiled. Round of applause. Well done you. What could be worse than that?'

'Plenty.' Jack pointed out of the window. 'For instance, there's a fire-breathing dragon in Queen Square.'

'Are you sitting comfortably, children? Then Missy will tell you the end of this strange story, and how it came to be that poor, dear Teddy Sparkles simply had to die ...!

'There was just no other way, you see, because, in reimagining the past the way he had, and taking us all back there, he had tangled everything up. Silly old Teddy Sparkles had conjured up a 1925 that was infused not just with his memories, but also with the stories he had heard the governess read to the children every night. He had absorbed her tales of dragons and phoenixes and walking scarecrows ... and so now London and the whole world was plagued with these peculiar beings ... Gorgons and harpies, angels and centaurs. They were everywhere and taking over this reality.

'"Teddy Sparkles, what have you done?" cried Esme, as the dragons came swarming in the skies over Queen Square, roasting the rooftops with emerald flames.

'"I've done it all wrong!" howled that idiot bear. "I've mixed up plain reality with awful whimsy ... and now there's chaos everywhere!"

'Oh, and children, it was quite true. There were savage, talking tigers bounding into Buckingham Palace and eating up members of the Royal Family. There were elephants with elephant guns in hot air balloons, taking pot-shots at people far below. It was as if these creatures of the imagination were seizing their chance to take revenge upon the humdrum world ...

'And there was I – Missy – forced to become the heroine of the hour, just as I often am in moments like this. Those children begged me. "Oh, Missy, you're so brave and beautiful. Only you can save the planet!"

'I listened to their flattery. And I watched the hordes of strange creatures wreaking havoc on 1925. I sat with the children, having tea at the British Museum, one glorious afternoon, and all the mummies had come to life and were dancing a conga out of the section devoted to Ancient Egypt. The café was a very exciting place to be because, as we sipped our tea, we could also see dinosaur skeletons stretching and heaving themselves into life, and doing battle with statues of gods from long ago. It was quite exciting, but also very, very noisy.

'"No one can rule over this soggy mess." I shrugged. "I suppose I will just have to help mankind. And to that end, children, I'm afraid Teddy Sparkles will have to die."

'"Oh no!" cried Esme, Jack and Peter. Well, Peter actually said "Boop!" of course, but it amounted to the same. "Please, don't hurt lovely Teddy Sparkles."

'He was there with us, the noxious beast. Sitting on our café table and looking like butter wouldn't melt in his mouth. And I was forced to explain once again that he wasn't just an innocuous-looking stuffed bear covered in glitter. Oh no. He belonged a race of wily reality-engineers from Ursino Six. His furry little paws had tampered with our timelines and only he could set things back on their correct course ...

"'Buy me some cakes and I'll consider it," he snapped.

"'You see, children," he sighed, as he pretended to eat cream cakes. "It's rather like when you draw a picture, and get it a bit wrong, and use your eraser to rub out the same aggravatingly wrong bit again and again. You know how the paper will go dirty and eventually tear?" He let a single tear roll down his furry cheek. "That's how it is with reality, too."

"'No, it isn't," I snapped. "I've messed about with the nature of reality enough to know it's more robust than that. What he means, children, is that, in setting your world of 1925 back to rights, he will deplete himself of his final stores of psychic energy. He will end up rubbing himself out of existence." I poured out more tea for us all, and all eyes were on Teddy Sparkles.

"'She's quite right," that troublesome bear quivered.

"'Teddy Sparkles, you can't die!" gasped Esme, and the others looked just as concerned.

'I said briskly, "Sometimes, in cosmic situations like this, then someone has to make a noble self-sacrifice. And, to be honest, it's only right and proper that it's Teddy here. And listen – the British Museum is falling down around our ears. Those monsters are getting out of hand. All the mummies and dinosaurs and everything are going to break out of here quite soon and go rampaging right across London ..."

"'I'd rather Teddy Sparkles was still here," said Esme. "As well as all the monsters and magical beasts. I like them."

"'Boop," said Peter.

'A pterodactyl came swooping out of the courtyard then, flapping its wings and trying to get at the cherries on my hat, and I was forced to fight it off with my umbrella. "Teddy Sparkles must die," I told them, in my most sweetly reassuring voice. "And then everything will be all right."

'The oldest boy, Jack, could see the sense in what I said. He was nodding grimly. "Missy is right. Teddy, I think you ought to take the world back to how it was … before you changed everything. It's only right."

'And so Teddy Sparkles hung his head. He had liked this world the way it used to be, and was rather ashamed of having caused a dreadful fuss. He gave a shuddering, remorseful breath, for now he had resolved to die and do right by the human race – and the end of my story was nearing. "Goodbye, children," he wept. "I'll make everything right, as you wish. But the effort will wipe me out of existence completely. I'll simply fade away before your eyes. It won't hurt much, I don't suppose, but I'll be gone and you'll never ever see me again …"

'Esme gasped and rushed to hold the tiny bear.

'"Oh, get on with it," I snapped and, in a fit of pique, I relinquished my narrating duties and threatened to vaporise his precious children if he didn't get a shift on.

'Teddy Sparkles glared at me. "You are the quintessence of wickedness, Missy. You really are."

'He always knew just the right thing to say, that Teddy Sparkles. And then he did a special magic thing and put the world to rights, vanishing in a flash, as he did so. Hurrah. The End.'

Except … it wasn't quite the end. Not for Missy and not for the children. Not quite yet.

'Come along, children,' said Missy, swinging her brolly happily as they left the museum. 'I'll walk home with you to Queen Square, laughing and jeering at you the whole way, pointing out all the horrible suffering and mess you've caused with your stupidity.'

And yet, they were all astonished to see that the rubble and destruction wrought by dragons and demons and talking statues had vanished utterly. London was bright and sunny that morning in spring. Everyone was behaving as if nothing untoward had happened at all.

'It's most peculiar,' said Esme, as they lagged behind Missy down those narrow streets.

'Reality is real once more,' said Jack. 'With his dying gasp, Teddy Sparkles gave us back our world.'

'Boop,' added Peter happily.

'And now we have to live our lives all over again,' said Esme in wonder. 'I can't really remember very much of mine, can you, Jack? It's all faded, like a queer dream, but I think there was a War and … and … No, it's all gone now …'

'This time perhaps we'll get to choose what we want to do with our lives without Missy's interference.'

Esme watched their governess pause before a sweetshop, her eyes glittering with greed. 'I do hope she'll leave us alone from now on. It's all been quite terrifying. Especially that rather bizarre part of the story when she started narrating.'

Jack shuddered. 'I hope she'll go, too. She's done enough damage.'

They became aware then that the sweetshop owner was engaging in conversation with Missy, and she was reacting violently and angrily to something he was saying. Now the man was laughing and she was fuming.

'What is it?' said Esme. 'She's not going to vaporise him, is she?'

The children drew closer in order to listen.

'Why, of course I know who you are!' the shop owner was chuckling. 'You're that lovely, magical governess from the famous stories, aren't you? You're a bit prickly and snooty on the outside, and sometimes you're downright deadly, but you've got a heart of gold really, deep down. Everyone knows that! Everyone knows who you are, Missy! You're famous!' He laughed out loud and started calling out to other passers-by. 'Look, look here! It's Missy! The famous governess who has all the magical adventures! Look, here!'

Soon there was a crowd gathering around Missy.

'She looks absolutely furious!' Esme laughed.

'This is all Teddy Sparkles' doing, I bet!' laughed Jack. 'He's engineered this reality. He's fixed it so that she can't creep about any more, getting up to nefarious schemes. That wily bear has seen to it that she's the one thing she doesn't want to be … famous!'

'And *loved*!' Esme chuckled. 'Look at her face! That's man's fawning all over her. She looks horrified!'

'Boop!' said Peter.

Missy was just about tearing out her hair as people gathered for autographs. Someone was holding up their squirming baby so she could kiss it.

'Ugh! I can't stay here!' she squawked. 'I'm surrounded by blithering ninnies!'

The crowd laughed at that. 'Ain't she a card? She's so abrasive! But she's all right underneath! She's got a kind heart …!'

'I don't have a kind heart!' Missy roared in frustration. 'Beneath this gorgeous bosom are beating *two* hearts of pure, unadulterated *evil*!'

But the crowd outside the sweetshop simply laughed even harder at her.

And so did the children.

Missy unfurled her umbrella quite savagely. 'Right! I'm leaving 1925 for ever!'

'Goodbye, Missy!' called Esme and Jack as she zoomed into the startling blue skies above Bloomsbury. Their younger brother cried 'Boop!' and the crowd gasped at her jet-propelled boots.

She shot into the air and shouted something extremely rude down at the lot of them.

The years unfolded once again, in many ways similarly to the way they had the first time round. The children got to choose their own destinies this time, which was much better and more agreeable all round, they thought.

Esme became a grandmother. She inherited the house in Queen Square and, one very snowy Christmas, she had all her children and grandchildren visiting.

Her favourite child was Jane, the youngest. Jane was quieter than the others, and often got elbowed aside in all the kerfuffle of a large family. Esme took a special interest in her and, that Christmas morning, sat with her as she opened her presents. As usual, Jane looked very serious and concentrated as she set about her task. The others were raging about the place, causing an unholy din.

At last, Jane was left with one final, beautifully wrapped parcel. 'Who's that from, darling?' asked Esme.

'It doesn't say,' Jane observed solemnly. She set about untying the ribbons, very carefully, and laying them to one side to use again later.

Esme watched with a strange, cold feeling deep in her stomach.

'It's a bear!' Jane cried. 'It's a rather old, golden bear. His face is a bit squashed and he's a little crumpled. But he's awfully nice. Look at him, Grandma Esme! Just look at his face! Oh, thank you. Thank you so much!'

'But … he isn't from me …' gasped Esme. 'Where did he come from?'

'Oh, look! He's covered in glitter,' said the child. She hugged him hard.

He turned to Esme and those topaz eyes stared into her own.

Then Teddy Sparkles quite distinctly winked at her, she was sure of it.

The Liar, the Glitch and
the War Zone
Peter Anghelides

Today ...

... St Mark's Square in Venice bustled with activity. Locals and tourists criss-crossed the piazza in happy, animated groups as preparations continued for the *Carnivale*. Lively children skipped beside their parents below the *Campanile*. Joyful couples held hands and peered into the cloudless blue sky. From their tall granite pedestals beside the waterway of the lagoon, Saint Theodore and a prancing unicorn gazed benevolently back down on them across the *Piazzetta*. Whichever way you turned, there were people full of love and energy and enthusiasm.

Missy hated them all.

She navigated a path between the granite pillars, studiously avoiding the pedestrian waves of excitement that lapped around her. If she didn't make eye contact, she could restrain her natural instincts, so long as they kept their necks out of breaking distance.

A human in a jaunty hat tested her patience with his eager tone as he foisted a printed flyer into her hand. There was a certain musicality about the Italian language that softened her reaction, so she accepted it instead of pushing him into the canal. The handbill was for an exhibition at the museum, with a photo of an item on display. Well, she was older than any of the exhibits, and much better preserved.

Tesori della laguna it read: Treasures of the lagoon. Missy considered dropping the handbill into the water behind her, and imagined it floating across the calm surface, then out into the 200-square-mile expanse of the lagoon itself. It would evade the gondolas and water taxis that ferried between the many Venetian islands, until it slipped past ocean-going liners and onward into the choppy waters of the Adriatic Sea.

Instead she crumpled it into her pocket, and took a brisk walk across the piazza. At least she could enjoy the crisp, clear air. Ahead of her, the Cathedral's Byzantine façade was masked by scaffolding, erected to enable renovations. Beneath one row of metal poles and wooden planks, there was an angry kerfuffle in the crowd.

'Gerald! My purse!' An English tourist wailed at her husband that someone had raided her handbag.

'Calm down, Felicity.' Gerald had an iPhone in one hand and a Hasselblad camera in the other. You couldn't tell whether he was more annoyed by the theft or that his attention had been wrenched away from photographing every square inch of the piazza.

Missy had already spotted the culprits – a tatty pair of children. The boy implored tourists to sign a petition, while the girl dipped into the victim's bag or pocket under cover of her conspirator's outstretched clipboard.

The boy now skulked in the gloom below the scaffolding, the clipboard clutched to his chest in feigned insouciance. The girl stood apart, and sucked on a nervous cigarette.

'Smoking is such a filthy habit,' declared Missy as she trotted up to them. 'It'll be the death of you. Unless furious Felicity –' here, she raised her voice and angled her head towards the sobbing victim – 'has Gerald beat you amateurs to death with his long and, let's be honest, over-compensatory lens.'

Felicity heard her own name, but took a moment to make the connection. Gerald hesitated with his Hasselblad.

The boy with the clipboard reacted faster. 'Antonia!' he yelled at his friend, and they scarpered before the tourists could react.

As she fled, Antonia had dropped a fat purse – evidently, the item she'd stolen from Felicity. Missy picked it up and put it in her own pocket.

'Where did they go? Gerald? Gerald!' Felicity's voice faded into the crowd as Missy walked towards the cathedral doors.

Fly-posted to a board on the scaffolding was an advert for the museum. *Tesori della laguna*, again – a collection of discoveries from lagoon excavation work beneath Venice. Like the handbill she'd stuffed into her pocket, the poster had a photo of an old candlestick, caked in mud and barnacles.

Missy squeaked a little laugh; if she wanted to see ancient history, she could travel there herself.

Well, she could if she managed to repair her TARDIS.

The calm darkness of the basilica's interior embraced her as she entered through the huge bronze doors. Adjacent signs declared that access to the cathedral was restricted during the renovation. Missy's heels rapped out an echoing announcement of her journey down the nave.

The huge gilded space was almost empty. As her eyes adjusted, Missy identified the two thieves at the far end of a row of chairs. They cowered, their heads down – asking for deliverance, or forgiveness, perhaps.

She strode past them until she reached the wood-panelled confessional further down the aisle. A soft glow suffused the area beyond it, a fluctuating rhythm of light that rippled across the dark space.

Missy turned to look at the grubby kids. 'Your prayers have been answered. Gerald's not the religious type. I'd wait here until he gets fed up. Maybe consider your sins.'

They scowled back at her.

'I'm just popping in here.' Missy tugged at the carved door of the confessional. 'May be a while. I've been a *very* naughty girl.'

And with a kick of her heel, she stepped through the door into her TARDIS.

Its landing in the basilica had been abrupt, and certainly unexpected, when …

Yesterday …

… she'd been escaping from a Gryphon combat unit.

That hadn't been the intention. Her fiendishly clever plan to elude the Daleks had incorporated a teleport, a flight of stairs, three bald lies, and a classical ballet routine. The subsequent leap into the Time Vortex should have been simply dazzling, but her *grand jeté* had ended up as more of a *pas de chat*.

How was she to know the Gryphon timeship was going to be there? Honestly, it had come out of nowhere. She hadn't seen a thing.

The TARDIS and the Gryphon ship shimmered and shuddered together in a ghastly temporal embrace. Well, that's what you'd expect if you tried to occupy the same physical space simultaneously at every point throughout eternity.

An incoming transmission sparkled into life as a holographic Gryphon made the introductions. They weren't polite. The creature had the body of a lioness, but with the wings of an eagle neatly folded across her back.

'Release this Gryphon vessel at once!'

It amused Missy to adjust the hologram so that it moved under her control across the TARDIS. She manipulated the image until the creature had a vase balanced on her head. It was the ugly green urn that

Missy hated but still displayed, because she'd stolen it on the day that Versailles opened, after Louis XIV had offended her with some now-forgotten slight.

'Do you have a name? I can't simply call you "Gryphon", now can I?'

The creature made a gruff sound low in her throat.

'I mean, it's like saying "Time Lord" or "human" or "Sontaran" or "mongoose" when you're talking to someone. And let me tell you, mongooses are dull company – always giggling away at their own private jokes.'

'Silence! I am the captain of this Gryphon ship—'

'Shall I call you Hermione?' Missy smiled as the vase seemed to wobble angrily. 'I'm more of a Slytherin girl myself. Always attracted to the bad boys. I can see a lot of Severus Snape in me.'

The Gryphon raised her paw to signal to someone out of shot. 'Charge the laser cannon.'

Missy wagged her finger, alarmed at this turn of events. 'Not such a smart move! We're in the Time Vortex. We need to back out of this with *great care*, not use firepower in the forever.'

The Gryphon ignored her, too busy acknowledging some response from her left. 'Very well. Fire at will.'

'You don't want to mess with me.' Missy scuttled around the TARDIS, flicking switches and checking gauges. 'I beat the Daleks.'

'I have no knowledge of these Daleks.'

Missy boggled. 'How can you not know about the Daleks? They're the most …' She considered the rising indicators across her controls. 'Oh, never mind.'

The first shot shuddered the whole room. Missy gasped at the force of it. 'I did warn you!'

The Gryphon captain gave a howl of surprise and rage. The ugly vase toppled off the hologram's head and smashed on the floor.

The second strike severed the communications channel. The hologram Gryphon fizzed out of existence.

The final blast scalded a hot trail of destruction that jounced and ricocheted down the timelines until it wrenched the two vessels out of their clumsy temporal grip.

Missy clasped her controls helplessly. They sizzled and sparked. Greasy smoke curled into the air and began to fill the room.

The TARDIS wheeled and whirled, and gouged a chaotic path out of the Vortex to crash-land in the basilica of St Mark's, Venice, where …

Now …

… Missy surveyed the damaged equipment across her control panels. The choking smoke had long dissipated, so it was safe to return. A slight fug still permeated the room, and there was an acrid aftertaste at the back of her throat.

She hitched up her skirt so she could crouch down below the control panels – inspecting, tweaking, disconnecting. A little heap of charred components piled up on the floor beside her. This could take some time ...

All the lights went out.

Missy groaned. She knew what had caused that. The primary power had leached out into the Vortex. The TARDIS couldn't dematerialise now – the pilot light had gone out, leaving no way to ignite the main energy source.

She scooped up the charred components from beside her, made a careful pile of them in her hat, and crawled on all fours through the dark to the exit.

Outside, the air was clearer, with the aromatic background note of incense. Light glimmered from the other side of the confessional box.

Missy straightened, and carried her hat full of components through to a side chapel. She propped her parasol by the altar, plonked the hat on its linen cloth, and began to examine the damaged items. A statue of Saint Michael peered down from beside her. The afternoon light that filtered from the stained-glass windows seemed to make his wings flutter in faint disapproval.

She studied her handiwork with satisfaction. Her repair of the dematerialisation circuit was fiddly, but ultimately successful. It stood on the altar, a delicate tetrahedron of complex equipment small enough to fit in her palm. Essential for operating the TARDIS. Much good that would do if the power wasn't restored.

'Excuse me, can I help you?'

A cross old woman squinted up from the altar rail. The nun's hands were fluttering in disapproval, too.

Her black habit reached the floor. Missy was reminded of an agitated Dalek.

'Maintenance work.' Missy ushered her away, to distract from the smudges on the linen altar cloth. 'I'll be done soon.'

The nun shied from her touch. 'I will check with the procurator.'

Missy watched her shuffle off. 'Bless you!'

A clatter nearby made her whirl round. The two young thieves had sneaked up to the altar, and were rummaging through her equipment with a hungry look. The boy held his clipboard in one hand, and in the other was the dematerialisation circuit.

The girl noticed that she'd spotted them, and shouted her friend's name. The boy jumped one way, and the girl skirted in an arc around Missy in the opposite direction.

Missy snarled, and lunged for the boy, but he slipped past her and around the corner. She snatched up her parasol and ran after him, her heels tapping an angry staccato on the cathedral floor.

He'd got as far as the confessional when the nun stepped into the aisle, and the boy staggered to a halt. The old woman clucked furiously, and hobbled away.

Missy had caught up now, and pointed her parasol's ferrule at the quivering boy. His back pressed against the confessional, and he edged sideways in search of an escape route.

'I said, consider your sins,' she admonished him, 'not commit more. Your friend called you Mario. Is your *papà* a plumber?'

A shake of the head. 'No *papà*. Mario like Mario Balotelli.'

Missy stared blankly.

'The footballer. People say I look like him.' Mario clutched his clipboard like a protective shield. 'Don't hurt me.'

Missy gave a hoot of laughter. 'I'm not going to hurt you. I'm not going to kill you, either, though that's usually much more fun.'

The ragged boy flinched, and his eyes widened. He hadn't even considered this possibility.

Missy clucked her tongue. 'I said that out loud, didn't I? Sor-reeee.'

She lowered the parasol and put it in the crook of her arm. Couldn't use it, in case she damaged the dematerialisation circuit.

Mario saw his chance. He pushed himself away from the confessional, and jumped around the corner, where that brightness suffused the area.

Missy leapt sideways to follow him. But the brightness had flared more brilliantly now, and made Mario into a stark silhouette. He flailed in desperation, and was abruptly jerked backwards into the light with a shriek and a series of slowly diminishing curses.

Ah, the musicality of the Italian language.

Missy was surprised to hear a hum from the confessional. The TARDIS had obtained a power boost from a Vortex void. How had she not noticed that before?

She seized a nearby candlestick and tossed it into the abyss. It was swallowed up at once. The light flared and the TARDIS hummed again.

A temporal rift!

Missy cast round for other items to jettison into the void. Hymnals, cushions, several chairs. Each vanished and generated a short pulse of energy. If it was to recharge the TARDIS, she'd need to push an enormous amount of stuff into it.

The old nun had seen what was happening, and shambled back to remonstrate.

Missy had no time to argue. She seized the front of the nun's habit and shoved hard. The old woman squeaked a little cry of dismay and tumbled into the void.

There was a horrified gasp from behind Missy. Antonia was staring in appalled disbelief. Missy snapped a hand out and seized the girl's wrist.

Antonia gasped. 'Please, *signora!*'

'*Signorina*, if you don't mind.'

Missy's mind was awhirl. How could she recover the dematerialisation circuit? 'That brat took it with him through the void, and who knows if that's survivable. When the TARDIS crash-landed out of the Time Vortex, it weakened the fabric of reality close to it. A glitch in time. A temporal portal …'

Antonia stared at her.

'Talking out loud again, wasn't I? Interior monologue. Must try to avoid that.'

A flutter of whispers echoed from the middle distance. Down in the apse, in front of the main altar, a huddle of nuns pointed in her direction. Too many to push into the Vortex void, that was for sure.

Missy tightened her grip on Antonia's wrist. 'I can't have you blabbing about temporal portals now, can I dear?'

'Don't hurt me! I'm just a little child.'

'In my experience,' said Missy, 'that makes it easier to hide the body.'

She yanked open the confessional, propelled Antonia into the gap, and slammed the door shut.

The nuns waddled down the aisle. At this rate, they'd be right next to her within a week and a half. Missy glanced at the TARDIS. She could leave, but perhaps the nuns would have an urge to confess something.

Missy hunted through her pockets, pulled out the museum handbill, and scribbled *GUASTO* on the back for an out-of-order sign. She was attaching it to the confessional when she noticed the crumpled image on the front.

She couldn't believe it.

Missy launched into a run. Her heels clacked all the way down the aisle, through the huge entrance doors, and into the piazza.

Outside, a street cleaner was attempting to remove the fly-poster from the scaffolding. She batted him away with her parasol, to get a better look.

The *Tesori della laguna* poster had changed too. The object in the photo was still caked in mud and barnacles. But it wasn't a candlestick any more.

It was her dematerialisation circuit.

*

Within the hour …

… Missy was looking at the real thing with a growing sense of despair. All that fiddly work to repair it, and now here it was encased in centuries of grime, behind glass, presented for gawking mediocrities in a museum exhibit of grimy bric-a-brac. Fat chance of *that* ever working again.

It had survived its journey *into* the past – and perhaps so had Mario. But even assuming she tracked it down and retrieved it, that was pointless unless she could power up the TARDIS pilot system.

A nearby tour guide was particularly keen to get himself murdered. The young man interrupted her train of thought with a tiresome monologue about where all the treasures on display had come from. Her interest perked up when he mentioned the dematerialisation circuit.

'… unusual decorative jewellery, possibly of North European origin—'

'A bit further than that,' she snorted.

'*Signora?*' His badge said he was Gabriele.

'*Signorina*,' she replied. 'Are you an expert on this jewellery?'

'I am but a humble guide.' Gabriele furrowed his pretty brow. 'You should ask the curator here. A *dottorato di ricerca*, who knows far more than me.' He gestured around the room. 'All these treasures were unearthed during tests and excavations being done beneath Venice.'

'What's the use?' said Missy. 'There'll be no saving Venice after the ice caps melt in … oooh, not long from now as the crow flies.'

Gabriele looked puzzled. 'We have a barrier now. Thanks to Ugo Esposito, the Venice Tidal Barrier protects our whole lagoon. Otherwise, at times like this, with the convergence of the *aqua alta* and a strong sirocco wind, the rising water would slowly drown Venice.'

Missy smiled. 'What if the water didn't rise slowly?'

Gabriele's loveable frown deepened. 'But it *is* rising.'

'I didn't say it isn't *rising*,' said Missy. 'I said, what if it didn't rise *slowly*?'

Later that day …

… she was on the water.

Missy had set out to where the lagoon met the Adriatic in a stolen speedboat, trilling operatically and thrilling at her long hair's battle with the wind and spray.

She visited each section of the barrier, left her calling cards, and then moved on to the next. It was obvious that she could feed the Vortex void next to the TARDIS with every last chair in the cathedral, or all the nuns she could lay her hands on, and it would never be sufficient to reboot her ship.

But a relentless rush of water coursing unchecked through the church and into the rift would certainly float her boat. The final thing that stood in her way, literally, was the Tidal Barrier. Remove that, and the water would surge in an unstoppable torrent from the Adriatic right across the entire lagoon.

Venice would be submerged, of course. But that wasn't a problem. There's a reason that TARDISes are watertight.

Missy sat primly on a seat in Ugo Esposito's office, and eyed him up. The chief engineer thought she'd come to inspect his accounts.

'Be a pet,' she said, 'fetch me an espresso. One part hot water to seven parts gravel. I've been gadding about all day, and I need a bit of a kicker.'

While Esposito was away, she placed her final device beneath the barrier's control suite, right behind his desk. Like the others, it was a cunning contrivance of her own design that used Time Lord tech – though she'd stopped using sentient validium connections, after too many of her contraptions criticised her wiring.

'I like that.' She indicated the framed *Tesori della laguna* poster on Esposito's wall as he returned with her drink. It was the photo of her encrusted dimensional stabiliser. 'D'you know what it is?'

'No idea,' he said. 'We recovered it encased in fourteenth-century sediment when we excavated Venice. The curator at the museum would know. Something of an expert, I'm told.' He paused. 'Would you like a water with your espresso?'

'No.' Missy took the cup from him and swigged it in one gulp. 'I think I'll be seeing quite enough water, thanks all the same.'

That evening …

… the museum was about to close, but Missy was still able to squeeze in an appointment.

The curator's office was an odd jumble of papers and artefacts. Bulging ring binders jostled with sculptures and goblets. A plague doctor's *medico della peste* mask hung from a peg. A triptych painting showed a view of Venice. Old and new books mingled on the shelves.

Missy closed the door. 'You took your time.'

'I'm a busy woman,' said the curator. 'Didn't my assistant tell you?'

Missy thought about the charred heap of ashes she'd kicked under the desk in the outer office. 'He wasn't chatty.'

'So, what d'you find so fascinating about …' The curator checked her paperwork. '… stolen goods in fourteenth-century Venice?'

'I'm writing a short story.' Missy affected a knowing look. 'It has a backdrop of illegal trade. I need to know where thieves did their deals,' she said. *To track down my stolen goods*, she didn't add.

'There are a lot of things to consider there,' said the curator. 'A buoyant economy sees Venice awash with money. That coincides with a surge in demand and the market is flooded with stolen items flowing through the city.'

Missy scowled. 'Can you help?'

The curator handed her a printout. 'Old school.'

Missy unfolded the paper. It showed a historical chart of Venice, with streets emphasised in highlighter pen. 'It certainly is. GPS coordinates would have been fine.'

'No, the thieves met in an old school. Or the Venetian equivalent of a school in that period, according to museum records. I've indicated the building for you on that map.'

The curator stood, as though to indicate their own meeting was now concluded, studying Missy as she might one of her exhibits. 'Good luck, *signorina*. I do enjoy this kind of research myself. It's a real trip into the past.'

Missy's hand was already on the door handle. 'You have no idea.'

The smell was what Missy noticed first as she re-entered the cathedral. Behind the musky aroma of church incense there was now a stink of decay.

The place was busier. Ragged vagrants shambled around the dark building. Missy avoided them as she returned to the confessional. Beside it, the Vortex void was larger. Its soft light swirled and coalesced and split again into luminous soft colours.

As soon as she opened the confessional door and stepped into the TARDIS, Missy detected another distinctive odour.

'Have you been smoking in here?'

Antonia shuffled across the darkened TARDIS, her frightened face pale in the half-light that spilled in from behind Missy. 'I thought you were never coming back. Please let me out.'

'All right.' Missy beckoned her through the confessional door and out into the aisle of the basilica.

Antonia's nose wrinkled at the smell. Missy swiftly hooked her around the elbow with the curved handle of her furled parasol, before pushing her around the corner of the confessional and into the Vortex void.

The girl uttered a dismayed little scream, and vanished into the whorl of soft colours.

Missy studied the nails on her free hand. Counted to ten. Then tugged on the parasol.

Antonia burst back into the aisle, and bumped into Missy. She hugged her, until she felt Missy tense up.

'Seems to be safe.' Missy detached herself from the girl.

Antonia was blinking with disbelief. 'I saw light and water and people! Is that where Mario is? We have to find him!'

The girl was interrupted as a grubby figure stepped out of the void behind her. His clothes were torn scraps, and beneath a filthy face his neck bulged with ugly blisters. Well, that explained what was wrong with all these other people in the cathedral: the Black Death. Fourteenth-century bubonic plague.

Missy stepped smartly aside as he passed. 'Two-way traffic! Come on, dear. Let's find your boyfriend.'

Fourteenth-century Venice …

… welcomed them with a bump. The other side of the void wasn't in the cathedral. Instead, it swirled and roiled in an alleyway that ran alongside a small canal.

Scattered candles and a wooden chair floated near the surface of the water. And was that a discarded wimple?

If anything, the stench from the canal was worse than in the cathedral. Despite the clear blue skies, Missy heard approaching thunder.

She unfolded her printout, and realised she hadn't got a clue where she was. 'No street signs in fourteenth-century Venice,' she told Antonia.

They cut across a small bridge into a main thoroughfare. A stream of people – men, women, beggars, merchants, nobles – ran in a panic towards them, stumbling, knocking each other over. Some went down and didn't get up again.

A spear of laser light seared down the thoroughfare, and Missy realised it wasn't thunder she'd heard. The light cut down the slower Venetians and showered the street with debris from buildings.

Two grotesque, leonine figures trotted along the opposite bank, and stopped to stare straight across at them.

'Lions.' Antonia's incredulous voice was barely a whisper. 'Lions with lightning.'

'Gryphon warriors,' snapped Missy. 'Big game hunt. And I'm the prey.'

Antonia clutched Missy's arm. 'They can't reach us from there.'

One of the Gryphons shook its long mane, flexed its shoulders, opened its wings, and took off towards them over the canal.

Missy shoved Antonia aside. 'Run!' she hissed. With any luck, the Gryphon would be drawn to the fleeing girl first, and she could avoid any personal unpleasantness. What did she have at hand to defend herself? Nothing that would stop this flapping feline. Not like that time she'd used her brooch to escape from a lecherous lungfish on Pomfret IV, where she'd deflated both his ego and his swim bladder.

Missy shrank back into the cover of a doorway. The Gryphon had shown no interest in her. A device in its paw scanned for a time signature.

With a rustle of soft wings, a female Gryphon landed beside him.

'Hermione!' breathed Missy.

'The time signature is near,' the warrior reported.

The Gryphon captain gave a curt nod. 'Then we shall soon have the technology to repair our timeship.'

Around the corner from Missy, Antonia unsuccessfully attempted to stifle loud sobs of fear. Too late to strangle her into silence, and the Gryphons were getting nearer ...

In the distance, Missy spotted a cohort of Venetian soldiers making stealthy progress in the shadow of buildings alongside the canal. Missy raised her parasol, and sent a sonic pulse the length of the street that made the nearest soldier yelp in alarm and pain.

The Gryphons wheeled around at the noise, and rose into the air for a better look. With their position revealed, the soldiers yelled and charged. The Gryphons responded, raining down a withering series of killing shots.

Missy beat a swift retreat in the opposite direction, and bumped into Antonia at the corner.

The girl dried her tears. 'Will those soldiers be OK?'

'Unlikely. They brought swords to a laser fight.'

'We must find Mario, before he gets hurt, too.'

Missy unfolded her printout. 'If we can work out where we are ...'

Antonia uttered a cry of dismay. 'Never mind your stupid map. We should just *ask* people!'

Missy's glare was as withering as a Gryphon attack. 'Excuse me, have you seen a boy who'll look like a famous footballer 700 years from now?'

'Oh, come on, *signorina!*' In any other circumstances, Antonia's contemptuous look would have got her killed. 'This is fourteenth-century Venice. He's black. He's wearing Reeboks and a Nice football shirt.'

They steered clear of the sporadic fighting and, between them, asked a succession of well-dressed merchants, ragged beggars, and armed soldiers if they'd seen an unusual-looking child. Missy's frustration built into a cold fury at the slow progress of having to ask idiot human strangers for help.

At last, as the freezing night closed in, a priest helped them narrow their search to a battered construction in the west of the city. An old school building. Finally, the curator's stupid map made sense.

'I'll check inside. Shout if any of those creatures appear.'

Missy strode down the street and in through a dilapidated doorway. It was a fleapit off a tired, forgotten square. She pulled on her gloves and negotiated broken wooden stairs that led up to an uncurtained room of exposed boards with a cramped row of single beds.

Mario was sprawled on one of the bare frames. His dead eyes stared at the ceiling, and his body was a mass of sores. On the floor beside him sat a lamp that contained an unlit, half-burnt candle.

Next to that, a sheet of paper on his battered clipboard was annotated in biro. A futile list of names of those who might be interested in his stolen goods. Before he'd got to any of them, the plague had got to him.

And standing on that scribbled sheet was the dematerialisation circuit.

As she descended the rickety stairs, Missy nearly collided with a dark-robed figure in a beaked mask. The plague doctor paused, and the mask's nose pointed at her as if in accusation.

'You're a bit late.' She scribbled a brief note on the clipboard as the doctor pushed past. Missy completed a more cautious descent of the staircase. 'Unless you're peddling miracle cures ...'

At the end of the street, Antonia was waiting. Missy saw the girl take a drag on a sneaky cigarette, drawing unwelcome attention from passers-by. She snatched it from the girl's lips, took a hungry drag herself, then spat out smoke and threw the thing in the filthy gutter.

Missy tugged her jacket straight. She could feel the reassuring shape of the dematerialisation circuit in the inner pocket. 'Come on. It's getting dark.' She lifted Mario's lamp, and lit the scrap of candle with Antonia's cigarette lighter.

'Didn't you find him?'

'He's gone.' Missy flourished the clipboard. 'But look! He left a wee note. *Vado all'altro mondo.*'

'The other world,' repeated Antonia. Her eyes glittered in the candlelight. 'He must have gone back home through that ... temporal portal!'

'And so must we.' Missy looked at the paper. 'Such neat handwriting.'

'He's the educated one, out of the two of us.'

Missy dropped the clipboard to the ground. 'You're telling me.' She set off down the dark street at a brisk pace. 'Hurry up, now. Long journey ahead. Hundreds of years, in fact.'

Now …

… they stepped out of the Vortex void. It had expanded to dominate the confessional, and cast its eerie colours across the whole basilica.

Missy dropped Mario's extinguished lamp by the TARDIS door, and trod a wary path to the opposite aisle. In the dappled light, the statue of Saint Michael seemed to wave his wings in an unfelt breeze. Slumped in chairs or sprawled in the nave, accidental escapees from fourteenth-century Venice had found their final rest seven centuries after their own time.

Venetian escapees weren't the only new arrivals. Because it wasn't the statue of Saint Michael that loomed into view from the side chapel. A Gryphon warrior had traversed the void ahead of them.

The warrior surged forward, his wings whipping up a fierce squall of air as he swooped across at them. He batted Antonia to one side, and spun to face Missy, blocking her access to her TARDIS. He pulled back his lips to reveal ferocious teeth, and his shattering roar reverberated around the whole basilica.

The Gryphon raised one massive paw, and for a moment Missy thought he would strike her down where she stood. But instead, he had lifted a comms device to his savage mouth. 'She's here, Captain.'

'I want her alive. But not necessarily unharmed.' Hermione's electronic voice crackled in the still air. 'I'm on my way.'

Muscles flexed under the warrior's fur as he bore down on Missy.

She brandished her parasol. 'What are you staring at, Aslan?'

He swatted it from her, and it rattled off into the distance.

Missy smiled her fiercest smile. 'C'mon. You're a bit of a pussycat, aren't you? Well, mostly pussycat, with a bit of budgie mixed in.'

The warrior reared back as a lit candle struck his head from behind, and the hair of his mane crinkled and burned. He spun around in a furious attempt to extinguish it.

Missy felt herself pushed forward. Antonia was steering them down the aisle to the exit in a frantic flight through the darkness, 'Come on!' She shoved the parasol back into Missy's hand, grabbed another offertory candle, and flung it at the warrior. 'We're getting out of here.'

The recovering Gryphon pounded through the cathedral. He caught up with them at the exit, intimidatingly large even as he folded his wings to pursue them outside.

Missy and Antonia heaved at the huge, ornate cathedral doors, and managed to close them on the warrior. Feathers scattered as one delicate wing crunched and crumpled between the carved doors.

The Gryphon bellowed a shattering roar of pain and anger, and fell back inside.

Missy hurried into the main square. 'That's why I never let my daughter have pets. Once they outgrow the house, you just have to put them down.'

Antonia wasn't listening. She stared in horror across the piazza.

Venice was in flames. Broken remnants of the *Carnivale* had scattered over the devastated space, bright clothes and masks trampled into damp ground and stained with blood. Ragged corpses slumped against the cracked columns of the *Biblioteca*. The bricks of the *Campanile* were scorched.

'Those lions aren't the only things that came through the rift,' gasped Antonia.

'People and plague.' Missy paused for breath. Running was so not her style. 'Time has moved on ahead of us here. And the big cats have been on safari.'

Around the corner she surveyed the *Piazzetta*. At the far end, the shattered combs of sunken gondolas jutted from the soiled lagoon. From his granite column, Saint Theodore looked down on the devastation. And above the other column, swooping over the unicorn statue and towards them out of the smoky sky, came Hermione.

Missy turned on her heel, and fled back into the square, desperate for cover. She flinched at the sudden, brutal chatter of automatic weapons – then laughed in delight when she saw a brace of Italian troops.

They emerged from the cover of the *Biblioteca* to fire at Hermione, who banked left to retaliate.

Missy and Antonia reached the piazza again. The cathedral doorway was now blocked by the Gryphon warrior, nursing his broken wing and an enormous grudge.

'No way back in.' Missy stamped her foot.

Antonia tugged her sleeve. 'Let's try something else.' She led them around the side of the cathedral, taking careful steps to avoid the scattered debris – abandoned bags, a staring corpse, the smashed remnants of a Hasselblad. Torn flaps of a museum fly-poster on the scaffolding featured a corroded candlestick.

Antonia grasped the rungs of a propped ladder. 'Up we go.'

'Up the scaffolding, you mean?' Missy bridled. 'Do I look like I'm dressed for mountaineering?'

'Do I look like I care?' Antonia held out her hand, and together they climbed the scaffolding.

The platform at the top ran alongside a large stained-glass window. Supplicant women knelt piously, and gazed up in their glazed adoration of an indulgent deity with a halo. Missy clucked her tongue.

Antonia ran her hands along the frame. 'It doesn't open.'

Missy wielded her parasol, and the lower window shattered in a rainbow spray of broken glass. 'It does now.'

Fragments tinkled onto the floor far below. It was a vertiginous drop into the dark. Missy stood on the parapet, popped open her parasol, and hopped through the gap.

'Wait for me!' squeaked Antonia, and jumped after her.

Missy tensed involuntarily as Antonia clung on. The parasol descent was somewhat faster than she'd have liked, and they landed on the basilica floor with quite a jolt.

'It's designed for one person.' Missy shrugged off her embrace.

Antonia's eyes narrowed in the gloom. 'You didn't think to use that to climb up the scaffolding?'

'Only does *down*, dear.' Missy snapped the parasol shut. 'It's a work in progress.'

A guttural growl echoed through the quietened cathedral. Far down the aisle, the Gryphon warrior struggled painfully in their direction. He loosed off a wild laser shot. The pulpit beside them exploded into flames, and its ornamentation melted into a pool of brass on the floor.

They scuttled across to the confessional, wrenched open the door, and threw themselves into the darkened TARDIS.

'Safe,' breathed Antonia.

'Trapped.' Missy attempted to drop her parasol into the umbrella stand, but a clattering noise told her she'd missed. 'Hey, this is no time for a cigarette!' Antonia had sparked up her lighter. 'Oh my?God, is this what human parenthood is like?'

Antonia's exasperated sigh almost blew out her lighter flame. She lit the old lamp she'd retrieved from outside. '*Human*. You said that earlier, too. Like …'

'Like I'm not? Oh, come on! Flying lions. Holes in time. Big space in a little box. Impossibly good-looking woman in couture clothing. Do keep up.'

Antonia considered this. 'At least it's brighter in this thing than when you locked me up.'

'Well, all those smellies coming through the tear generate Vortex energy, and the TARDIS just soaks that up. Ooh … Maybe not trapped, after all.' Missy looked at the control gauges. 'Could you flick that switch, dear?'

Antonia reached across the panel and did so – then shrieked as a lightning spark of blue-white energy illuminated the whole room and made her leap a foot into the air.

'Yes,' noted Missy. 'It does seem like power has got through. That should be enough.'

Antonia sucked her burned finger. 'Enough for what?'

'Remote activator. Wireless.' Missy waggled a control box in the air. 'It's all the rage.'

She pressed the button.

The transmat packs that Missy had placed earlier all activated simultaneously. In the blink of an eye, whole sections of Ugo Esposito's Tidal Barrier flipped out of existence and reappeared at random a mile and a half away.

The waiting water of the Adriatic saw its opportunity, and surged through the abrupt breaches in the barrier in a catastrophic failure of the defence system.

Klaxons hooted a futile warning in the chief engineer's control suite. The facility quivered and rattled around Esposito as the water approached. His framed museum poster, showing an encrusted candlestick, dropped off the wall. That was the last thing Esposito saw before Missy's bomb went off under his desk.

The *aqua alta* gushed unchecked in a tsunami that raced across the lagoon. Speed boats were thrown into the air like scraps. A cruise ship took a violent lurch to one side, throwing deckchairs and occupants overboard. *Vaporetti* vanished as if vaporised.

The raging sea reached Venice. It streamed across St Mark's Square, and engulfed everything in its way – plague victims, soldiers, Gryphon warriors, street furniture from restaurants, the detritus of the *Carnivale*. The scaffolding around the cathedral collapsed into a cacophonous chiming heap of tangled metal.

The tide carried its grim cargo through the main entrance and across the basilica. Pews and prayer books, candles and corpses washed down the nave towards the confessionals.

The glowing maw of the Vortex void expanded to swallow it all, glowing brighter and fiercer.

The TARDIS lights flickered on. Missy watched Antonia's reaction as the shadows melted away to provide her first proper look at the cavernous interior. The girl blinked into the light that spilled down from the arched roof's recesses, higher even than the basilica outside. Was that astonishment or fear in her eyes?

'This place ... What's happening?'

'Hush, dear, *mamma* is working.' Missy retrieved a small mechanical item from her pocket and blew fluff from it. 'Dimensional stabiliser. Let's pop that into place. You know, I really should get a spare.'

Antonia wasn't really listening. She stared open-mouthed at a succession of images displayed on the screen. Venice was awash. Buildings and vessels and people alike were being consumed by a merciless torrent of filthy ocean water. Now, *that* was fear in her eyes.

Missy focused on the controls. 'I have enough power to enter the Vortex. But the Gryphons can follow through that rift as easily as I can, and that leads them straight to me.'

'What about Venice? Don't you care that ...'

'I've burned through whole star systems faster than you can light a cigarette!' spat Missy. 'Now, the photo on that poster changed back to a candlestick ... Proof that changes through the void *can* correct. So I'm going back into the Vortex so I can time-ram my TARDIS. Bump it out of the way, and prevent its original collision with the Gryphon ship. Now, hold on tight. This is *dangerous*.' She seized the console. '*Dangerous* is English for *pericoloso*.'

The display screen showed vessels converging in the swirling chaos of the Time Vortex ... the TARDIS ... the Gryphon timeship ... and the TARDIS again ...

The discordant shriek of the engines filled the air around them. Missy committed the coordinates, and hung on for dear life.

*

A beady eye glittered disapprovingly from the other side of the TARDIS. But it was only the stuffed raven she'd once crudely stapled to the arm of a Queen Anne chair.

Missy got up from the floor and straightened her hat. The control gauges confirmed that the time-ram had worked.

'No original collision with the Gryphon timeship means the TARDIS never crash-landed. No crash-landing, no Vortex void. And *evanesco* for Hermione!'

Antonia hauled herself onto the chair, her eyes red from weeping. 'Venice is destroyed. It's all gone.'

'It never happened. Everything's back in its right time zone.'

Antonia calmed down a little. 'Mario! His note said he was coming home. Let's find him!'

Missy frowned. 'Don't you feel some things are best left in the past? Old boyfriends. The Black Death. Mr Blobby?'

'Where is he?'

'Give him a him a couple of weeks, and look him up on Facebook.'

Antonia jumped to her feet in anger, and gestured around her. 'You must be able to find him, with all ... this. I want to see him!'

Missy tutted sympathetically, her eyes glittering. 'I can arrange that, my pet.'

Fourteenth-century Venice ...

... was not what Antonia had expected to see when the *signorina* ushered her out. She stepped through the doors, and from behind a tapestry too gaudy for the room in which she now found herself.

A commotion outside drew her to the window. She wiped grime from the cracked pane with her sleeve, and peered into the street.

At the far end, she was astonished to see ... herself in conversation with the *signorina*. But surely the *signorina* was in that large, bright room behind the tapestry?

Antonia started back across to it, but stumbled over a dilapidated bedframe that protruded from the darkened corner. In the half-light, she could make out a sprawled figure on the bed. Hot bile rose in her throat, and she stumbled away from the broken body.

Mario. *Vado all'altro mondo.*

A commotion across the room startled her. She watched in bewilderment as the tapestry rippled and faded away, revealing a bare wall.

She rushed to the window. The dark street was empty.

Antonia collapsed to the filthy floorboards and burst into bitter, hopeless tears.

Today ...

... St Mark's Square in Venice bustled with activity. Locals and tourists criss-crossed the piazza in happy, animated groups as preparations continued for the *Carnivale*.

Time had reset itself. The Gryphon timeship never crashed in fourteenth-century Venice. The catastrophic twenty-first-century flood never happened. None of the tourists or waiters or police who scuttled about the city would remember it, Missy realised; they'd not been in contact with active TARDIS technology the way she had. Her and that girl, whatever she'd been called.

Saint Theodore looked down at Missy from his granite column. On the adjacent pillar, the stone statue of a winged lion stared at the horizon.

The TARDIS looked like a bookcase when it landed in the museum library.

Missy spent a while reading through historical accounts, to confirm that there was no record of Gryphons in Venice's past. Just an echo of them in the image of a winged lion. She was safe from the wretched things now.

She left the dusty volumes and manuscripts on the library desk, and went back to the TARDIS. A scrawny figure was studying the contents of the bookcase. Missy was startled to see that it was that girl again ... Antonia, that was her name.

'I wasn't expecting to see you again, dear.'

Antonia glared. 'If it wasn't for her, no one would *ever* have seen me again. And Mario ...' Further words choked her. She stuffed a note into Missy's hand and stalked away.

The note was from the museum curator. Missy skimmed it: two short paragraphs of neat handwriting chastised Missy for her lack of caution, and told her that she would need to try much harder.

Outrageous nerve, thought Missy. Who did the little insect think she was?

Filled with fresh indignation, Missy found her way to the curator's office. She breezed through the outer room, ignored the assistant, and burst through the door without knocking.

The office was empty. No books, no binders, no curios. A single carnival outfit hung on the hat stand: a plague doctor's beaked costume.

In the outer office, the assistant glanced up from his desk. The rollback of reality had restored him to life, but Missy was perfectly prepared to make him a powdery pile of cinders again if necessary. 'All right. Where is she, your boss?'

'I really couldn't say,' he smiled. 'As you can see, she has gone.'

It was clear he had no more information, and could only repeat to Missy: '*La dottoressa non funziona più qui* … The doctor doesn't work here any more.'

Girl Power!
Jacqueline Rayner

Dear Doctor,

Here is this week's list of requests, for your approval (or otherwise):

1 x can extra-strength hairspray.

Book on the history of 'this ridiculous planet, let's see why he likes it so much'.

Some of those sugar mice with string tails. (Because 'you can dangle them by the tail and bite them and it feels like you're eating something alive.' I pointed out that this was not necessarily behaviour of which you'd approve, and she said, 'Why not? I always imagined that was why he was so fond of jelly babies.')

Yours sincerely,
Nardole

N. Yeah, go on, she can have
all of that. D

Sir, I was expecting you to deny that thing about the jelly babies. N

> N. Really? I have to deny things now?
> Show a little faith! D

You still haven't actually denied it. N

*

Your Andromeda.gal.ax order #ZZ9-ZZZ-B
Delivery Update

Hello Mr N A Rdole!
We're going to deliver your package today.

If nobody's available to accept the delivery, we'll leave it in your preferred time zone if you've selected alternative galactic coordinates under preferences. Otherwise, if possible we'll teleport the package to a nearby life form that has reached an appropriate place on the evolutionary scale.

Delivery Information:
History of the World (hardback) by T.B. Dryden-Butler.

This is the final part of your order. Your order is now complete.

*

Dear Doctor,
Here is the latest list of requests, for your approval or disapproval:

1 x mascara (black, volumising).

Some more sheet music. Something classical (Bach, Beethoven, Stormzy).

A book on the history of this ridiculous planet 'that actually has some women in it'.

A bag of marshmallows.

A small campfire (for toasting the above).

Yours sincerely,
Nardole

> N. No to the campfire. If she's still got that can of hairspray, we could be in big trouble.
> The rest is OK. D

*

Your Andromeda.gal.ax order #ZZ9-ZZZ-C
Delivery Update

Hello Mr N A Rdole!
We're going to deliver your package today.

Thank you for updating your delivery preferences. We have noted that you have updated your taxonomic profile to indicate that we are not to leave parcels with members of the kingdom Plantae (hereafter referred to as 'plants'). We apologise for the error. We have corrected our system to indicate 'plants' are not the major intelligent life forms on planet Earth.

Delivery Information:

'Lovely Lovely Lashes' (midnight black).
The Girls' Big Book of Historical Women (paperback)
   by Mirabelle Dolby.

This is the final part of your order. Your order is now complete.

*

Dear Doctor,
This is what she's come up with this week, for you to say yay or nay:

1 x pack blister plasters. Apparently wearing heels all the time is murder on your feet, but neither of us would know that as we're just pathetic men with no understanding of what women suffer.

A packet of liquorice whips. Or actual whips. Or liquorice whips that are big enough to be used as actual whips.

A book on women in the history of this ridiculous planet 'which isn't just about who they're married to'.

A tiger.

Yours sincerely,
Nardole

N. Yeah, that's OK. D

Actually, second thoughts, not the tiger.
It wouldn't be fair on the tiger. D

Dear Sir,

Aaargh! Already ordered it!
N

*

Your Andromeda.gal.ax order #ZZ9-ZZZ-D
Delivery Update

Hello Mr N A Rdole!
We're going to deliver your package today.

Thank you for updating your delivery preferences. We note that we are also not to leave parcels with members of the kingdom Fungi (hereafter referred to as 'fungi') and have noted that you consider the kingdom Animalia (hereafter referred to as 'animals') to be the dominant life forms on planet Earth, despite all evidence to the contrary.

Delivery Information:
Great Women in History (hardback) by E. Smythe (Dr).
Panthera tigris, subspecies 'Siberian Tiger'.

This is the final part of your order. Your order is now complete.

*

Your Andromeda.gal.ax order #ZZ9-ZZZ-D
Update

Hello Mr N A Rdole!

We have processed your requested refund for the following item:

   Panthera tigris, subspecies 'Siberian Tiger'.

Please teleport the item in unused condition to any depot in your nearest spiral arm within five working planetary rotations. Thank you.

*

ST LUKE'S GAZETTE
FOWL PLAY!

Seven chickens belonging to the university chaplain disappeared mysteriously overnight. "They were shut in at night as usual and I padlocked their coop," the Rev D. Thorne told us. "But in the morning they'd all gone. I had to have Rice Krispies instead of eggs for breakfast." There was no sign of any break-in. Anyone with any information is asked to get in touch with campus security.

*

Dear Doctor,
This is the new list, awaiting your approval:
   A packet of acid drops.
   500ml mercury.
   3 x azimuth sprockets.
   A book on smashing the patriarchy.

Yours sincerely,
Nardole

N. Oooh, acid drops. Haven't had those for centuries.
Could you get me some too? D

*

Your Andromeda.gal.ax order #ZZ9-ZZZ-E
Delivery Update

Hello Mr N A Rdole!
We're going to deliver your package today.

Thank you for updating your delivery preferences. We note that if you are not available when we attempt to deliver, we are to leave parcels only with members of the species Homo sapiens ('human'). However we would like to point out that the species Gallus gallus domesticus ('chicken') not only shares sixty per cent of its DNA with Homo sapiens, its population also outnumbers the humans by almost three to one on planet Earth, so it was quite frankly a very easy mistake to make. Also, in our view, it was the responsibility of the chickens to have a clearly visible sign stating that they did not wish tigers to be teleported into their dwelling. However we have agreed to replace the chickens as a good-will gesture.

Delivery Information:
2 x Acid drops (220g).

This is the final part of your order. Your order is now complete.

*

ST LUKE'S GAZETTE
FOWL PLAY – AGAIN!

The campus was terrorised last night by what witnesses have described as "seven robotic chickens with laser eyes and guns". Lecturer in Almost Everything, the Doctor, whom several witnesses claimed they saw chasing the chickens, told our reporter, "Just go home and have a biscuit or whatever it is you humans like to get up to on a Wednesday night." Our reporter tried to contact university chaplain Rev D. Thorne to see if there was any connection between the appearance of these avian automatons and the disappearance of his chickens a few days ago, but found only a slightly smoking hat just outside the hen run. The Doctor, who coincidentally had also come to visit the chaplain, shouted, "Nothing to see here!" as he backed out of the chaplaincy garden, adding, "Squawk, squawk, zap, squawk, I don't know what you thought you heard but that was definitely me squawking just now." Anyone with any information is asked to get in touch with campus security.

*

Your Andromeda.gal.ax order #ZZ9-ZZZ-E
URGENT RECALL

Dear customer,
It has come to our attention that certain carbon-based life forms have been mistakenly supplied

with Acid drops (200mg) containing sulphuric acid rather than citric acid. If this applies to you, please do not ingest any of the contents and return for a full refund. If you have already ingested the contents, please see the section 'Accidental harm, mutilation, dismemberment or death liability disclaimer' in our FAQ.

We apologise for any inconvenience this may cause.

*

Dear Doctor,
I am frankly quite sure she knew about the acid drops. She probably slipped them into the supply chain a couple of bodies back. I am also sure she knew that the tiger delivery would cause trouble and keep you distracted while she gets on with whatever she's really up to. Here are the latest requests, for you to approve or DISAPPROVE:

Sherbet lemons.
A helmic regulator.

Yours sincerely,
Nardole

N. All approved. D

Sir, you did notice how I said 'or DISAPPROVE', didn't you? N

N. I am capable of discerning nuance in the written word, yes. I don't know what your problem is with sherbet lemons. D

Sir! A HELMIC REGULATOR! That means travel through the Time Vortex!

N. Not necessarily. Just something to do with time. I'm interested to see where she's going with this. Just keep an eye on things. D

Dear Sir,
I have been trying to 'keep an eye on things', but this morning she told me that I had very pretty eyes and wouldn't they make a nice pair of earrings, so perhaps I should keep them to myself for a while if I didn't want to tempt a girl. Which I think might have been her way of hinting she didn't want to be watched so much.

Yours in some considerable trepidation,
Nardole

Interesting. That suggests her plan is near to fruition. Let's give her her head for a while, see where she's going with this.

Dear Sir,
I note your suggestion to 'give her her head for a while', an expression which I see is related to loosening a horse's reins. While fully appreciating your proposal,

I would like to propose an alternative course of action, which is STOP HER STOP HER NOW WHATEVER SHE'S DOING PLEASE I'M BEGGING YOU. I would also like to casually mention another Earth saying about horses, namely: 'There's no point shutting the stable door after the horse has bolted,' and to make it extra clear I will point out that by 'horse' I mean 'Missy', and by 'bolted' I mean 'destroyed this entire planet'.

Yours pleadingly,
Nardole

> Nah, she's not going to do that. Don't panic. D

D. I wish I had your confidence. N

*

INVITATION

Dear Marie Antoinette
You are invited to join MADAM (Missy's Army for the Demotion of All Men).

It shouldn't be 'let them eat cake', it should be poison the cake and give it to your husband, take over as ruler of France, guillotine anyone who doesn't like it. Simple.

RSVP

Your friend,
Missy

INVITATION

Dear Boudicca

You are invited to join MADAM (Missy's Army for the Demotion of All Men).

Like your style. Have you ever heard of the AK-47? I can supply.

RSVP

Your friend,
Missy

INVITATION

Dear Messalina

You are invited to join MADAM (Missy's Army for the Demotion of All Men).

You go girl! Hint: get a dog collar. Kinky and good for neck protection.

RSVP

Your friend,
Missy

INVITATION

Dear Eleanor of Aquitaine

You are invited to join MADAM (Missy's Army for the Demotion of All Men).

Fab stuff with the Fair Rosamund and the cup of poison/dagger thing. I'm going to nick it. Hope you don't mind. Of course if you do mind – I'll offer you a choice …

RSVP

Your friend,
Missy

INVITATION

Dear Florence Nightingale
You are invited to join MADAM (Missy's Army for the Demotion of All Men).

The Lady with the Lamp? Yawn yawn. Try the Lady with the Anti-Tank Missile. Or the Lady with the Grenade Launcher. And surely you've got access to some bio-weaponry? Scrape off a few smallpox scabs or something. Come on!

RSVP

Your friend,
Missy

*

Sir! This is most urgent! Acid! Mercury! Azimuth sprockets! And most obvious of all, sugar! Why didn't we see it before? I don't think I need to tell you how all those things combine with a helmic regulator – she has built a two-way space-time telegraph with time-scoop facility and is literally burning holes through the continuum! I've discovered she's contacting women from throughout history and trying to get them to rebel – this morning I intercepted self-returning trans-temporal acceptances from

Catherine the Great, Marie Curie, and all of Henry VIII's wives! I recommend IMMEDIATE removal of all privileges.

Yours in even more worry than before,
Nardole

> N. I think it's important to know where she's going with this. What her ultimate goal is. You're obviously a keen student of human idiom; have you heard the expression 'give her enough rope …'? D

Dear Sir, Is that the expression that goes 'give her enough rope and she'll tie you up, escape and probably destroy the universe'? N

> N. Don't be silly. D

*

MADAM: Mission Statement

Dear XX chromosome humans,
My name is Missy and I am much, much cleverer than you, but because I am also a woman at the moment, we have a bond. (A bond is apparently 'a force or feeling that unites people' and nothing to do with handcuffs. Sad face.)

It has come to my notice that being a woman isn't just about the addition of some wobbly bits and a sudden inability to grow a goatee. Apparently throughout the history of this ludicrous rock (offence intended), the addition of a Y chromosome is bizarrely seen as somehow 'better'. So we're going to do something about it, poppets. First we get rid of the stinky old patriarchy in a few teeny-tiny bloody revolutions, then we take over the world. Okey-dokey, everyone? My general advice would be to kill all men, but I suppose it's all right if you want to keep a few as pets. Or decorations. Or kitchen utensils.

Actually, second thoughts, probably not a lot of fun ruling the world if you don't have anyone to lord it over. I'm imagining maybe a tournament, men versus gorillas, men versus sharks, men versus spiny anteaters. The winners get to survive, hurrah! Also they can do all the housework and bake cupcakes and it'll be the law to tell them they're rubbish at parking.

'Why me?' you're probably asking. Well, mainly it's because I've read about you in a book. Yes, you end up in books, there's no need to get big-headed about it. But you're either already delightfully violent or in positions close to power, so I've chosen you as my little team, yay! Further instructions to follow.

Love and snogs,
Missy

PS. Babies. I understand that for some unfathomable reason, on this planet women grow sprogs inside of them and then just pop them out one day, along with half their internal organs and a bucket of slime. This is a ridiculous system. Change it.

*

Dear Doctor,
You really need to read the attached. She's advocating mass murder! Androcide! Or slavery, or something! What if some of these women take her up on the idea? The whole of history could be changed!

Yours close to panic,
Nardole

> N. Oh, she's just messing with them. There's almost no chance of any permanent damage to the time lines. D

Dear Sir, there's almost no chance of anyone being killed by a tortoise dropped by an eagle, but you try telling that to the playwright Aeschylus. N

> N. We don't talk about Aeschylus. Look, I tried to save him. I dressed up as a soothsayer and did all this 'Beware falling objects' business, but he got it into his head that meant he'd only be safe outdoors, and before I could convince him otherwise, the tortoise had landed. D

*

MADAM: Some Helpful Responses

It seems there are various annoying things that men say to women a lot. Some of these have been said to me. I have, of course, instantly vaporised the sillies, but you may prefer the subtler approach. Here are some ideas of how to respond if they are said to you.

IDIOTIC MAN SAYS: 'You'd be prettier if you smiled.'
RESPONSE: Ask him if he's heard of a 'Glasgow smile'. Produce your cut-throat razor. Demonstrate the Glasgow smile. Tell him he's now much prettier. Maybe sprinkle some glitter around just to make sure.

IDIOTIC MAN SAYS: 'You must be a witch.'
RESPONSE: Summon a demonic entity. While he's distracted by the demonic entity, burn him at the stake. Don't forget the marshmallows.

IDIOTIC MAN SAYS: 'I thought you were on a diet.'
RESPONSE: Stuff seven chocolate cakes down his throat, a Mars Bar up each nostril, turn his intestines into spaghetti, make spaghetti carbonara, eat.

IDIOTIC MAN SAYS: 'Calm down, dear.'
RESPONSE: Stay calm. Stab him.

*

Sir, this stuff is still very murdery. N

> N. Keep watching. We need to know her exact plan. No one will get murdered. D

Sir, I hate to disagree with you, but we're talking about a person who has turned entire planets into fireballs just to get enough light to put on her eyeshadow. N

N. She's changing her ways. D

D. I wish I was as sure of that as you are. N

*

MADAM: Things Women Aren't Allowed to Do

At various points in your history, women have been forbidden to do certain things. Here is some advice if you find yourself in any of these situations.

TOP TEN THINGS WOMEN AREN'T ALLOWED TO DO AND WHAT TO DO ABOUT IT:

1. VOTE
    Solution: Get a very short pencil and put a cross next to the candidate's name. I'm sorry, that should have read, get a very short pencil and use a cross**bow** to fire it at the candidate's brain. Tip: aim for the eyeball. It'll go right through. Squidgy jelly fun.
2. JOIN A GOLF CLUB
    Solution: Select a 9 iron. Then insert it (see diagram 43).

3. BECOME POPE

   Solution: Become Pope anyway. Oh, all right, you can disguise yourself as a man if you like. Just don't give it away by giving birth during a procession (I'm looking at you, Joan). Maybe do some stabbing as well, just in case.

4. GET ON A BOAT

   Solution: Apparently it's unlucky. Prove those sexist sailors right by blowing them all away with a machine gun.

5. SUCCEED A PARENT AS MONARCH IF THERE ARE ANY MALE HEIRS

   Solution: Slaughter all male heirs. Slaughter the monarch before he can have any more male heirs. Become monarch.

6. RIDE A BICYCLE

   Solution: Get two men. Tie their hands to their ankles. Join with a bicycle chain. Stick a saddle on one and handlebars on the other. Cycle merrily away. Don't forget to ring your bell!

7. DIVORCE THEIR HUSBAND

   Solution: Oh, honey, why would you even contemplate divorce in the first place when there's arsenic in the world? Strychnine's good too, they make really funny faces and a sort of 'bleerughaargheeek' noise.

8. OWN PROPERTY

   Solution: Someone or other once said that all property is theft. So steal the property. Then kill whoever thought it wasn't your property in the first place.

9. COMPETE IN OR WATCH THE OLYMPICS
   Solution: Set up your own games. Make them sound really super sexy. Let the men beg to be allowed to watch. Let them in. Then let those javelins fly!

10. ACT IN THE THEATRE
    Solution: Thank your lucky stars, girlies. Who'd be an actor?

*

Sir!

This morning I intercepted an order for 47 extra-smartphones, each to be sent to a different part of Earth's history – Ancient Troy, the Wild West, fifteenth-century France. What's she up to now?

I know you said to give her enough rope, but she's turning history into some sort of temporal cat's cradle!

Yours even more worried now, and if you recall, I was pretty worried already,

Nardole

N. I'm not stopping her just when it's getting really interesting! I think the outlines of her plan are starting to appear. She's never shown much interest in Earth's history before. Well, there was the time that she pretended to be a French knight in order to prevent Magna Carta being signed. I don't know why. I think mainly because she liked the beard. Ginger. Oh, and the time she tried to hijack a meeting of scientists that George Stephenson set up. I don't know why. Something about making the Earth a powerbase. Didn't make a lot of sense. Let's not even start on the Atlantis muddle. So this sudden interest – it's got to be going somewhere. Somewhere major. Probably connected with universal domination. You are my eyes and ears! Keep watching and listening. D

*

SPACEBOOK PROFILE

NAME: The Mistress
JOB: Sparkly happy good fairy at The Doctor's Happy Happy Vault of Niceness
NICKNAME: Missy
OTHER NAMES: Professor Thascales, Colonel Masters, Reverend Magister, Sir Gilles Estram, Mister Saxon. Look, if I called myself 'Reggie' or 'Dave' the Doctor never even had the decency to suspect it was me. I used to go to a lot of trouble dressing myself up for him so is it so wrong to want some attention?
CURRENT CITY: Bristol. I have absolutely no plans to wipe it off the face of the Earth with a tactical nuclear strike and anyone who claims otherwise is a liar, liar, pants on fire.
RELATIONSHIP: I don't even know what that is.

FAVOURITE QUOTE: 'I only need two things. Your submission and your obedience to my will.'

LIFE EVENTS: Born, Died, Died, Died, Died, Died, Died, Died, Died, Died, Died, Died, Died, Died, Took over some bloke's body, Died, Died, Died, Became a human, Stopped being a human, Died, Died, Became a woman, *Ruled!*

*

D. Now she's set up an account on Spacebook! N

> N. Could be interesting. By the way, thanks for the extra-smartphone. D

D. I haven't sent you an extra-smartphone! It must be some sort of trap! N

> N. Nope, definitely from you. D

*

SPACEBOOK – CREATE NEW GROUP

Name Your Group: MADAM

Add Some People:
Joan of Arc
Lady Jane Grey
Agrippina the Younger
Annie Oakley
Pocahontas

Lady Godiva
Agatha Christie
Mata Hari
Elizabeth Tudor
Nell Gwyn
Helen of Troy
Mary, Queen of Scots
Mary Tudor
Lucretia Borgia
Grace O'Malley
(You can add more later)

Personalise your invitation with a note:

Let's get down to business. We need to discuss how YOU can change the world. With a little help from your new BFF, Missy!

Select Privacy: Top Top Top Top Top Top Top Top Secret.

*

D. This looks like her next move. She's sent out several batches of invitations, all to women. N

N. Can you get hold of one of those extra-smartphones for me? I think I need to supervise this personally. D

D. I've ordered one for you. Should arrive three hours ago. Ohhhhh, I see. N

N. Just thank your lucky stars I remembered I needed to ask you to order it for me. It could have turned out like the curling tongs/badger incident. D

I won't mention Aeschylus again if you keep quiet about the curling tongs/badger incident. I still get nightmares. N

*

MISSY has started a conversation.

MISSY: Welcome, girlies! Let's take over the world!

GRACE O'MALLEY: Sounds good to me!

MISSY: Now, I know killing men is something that we all like to do for fun, but because I have been told very definitely that it's slightly naughty, my proposal is that we only kill men when it's really, really necessary, like if they stand between us and the throne to a kingdom, or if they spill our pint. OK?

LUCRETIA BORGIA: Spoilsport.

JANE AUSTEN: I beg your pardon, Madam, but think I may have been added to this group in error. Indeed, I have no desire to kill a man, be he ever so proud, miserly, or deceitfully inclined to lie about his marital or financial prospects in a way that would cause much pain and injury to a dear friend or sister of mine.

MISSY: It's a truth universally acknowledged that you need a kick up the backside, then.

JANE AUSTEN: I pray, do not turn such cruel words upon me.

MISSY: I'll turn something on you all right.

JANE AUSTEN has left the group.

MISSY: Well. Anyone else want to wimp out like Miss Regency Knickers?

AGATHA CHRISTIE: I'm not really sure what I'm doing in this group.

MISSY: Oh, come on! You've probably bumped off more people than anyone else here, maybe Bloody Mary excepted, and I have to say, you do it in style. Not afraid to sign your name to it, either. That's my kind of gal.

AGATHA CHRISTIE: But I only kill people in fiction!

MISSY: Fiction? What fun's that? You need to get your hands dirty. Feel the blade slipping in, watch the cheeks turning blue …

AGATHA CHRISTIE: I think you need help.

MISSY: Well, of course I need help! I'm locked up in a vault! I can't do it all myself. That's the whole point of this group!

AGATHA CHRISTIE: This is obviously some sort of joke, but I don't understand it. Goodbye, ladies.

AGATHA CHRISTIE has left the group.

MISSY: What a pair of wusses.

BOUDICCA: Put all men to the sword!

MISSY: That's the spirit!

MESSALINA: I don't want to kill all men. Not the pretty ones. Or the rich ones. Or the ones with really big muscles. And, you know, the ones with those gorj smooth chests that can be oiled up and you can run your hands all over …

MISSY: That's all right, I've said we can keep a few. Anyway, it's mainly kings and emperors we want to mash. Let's start with Henry VIII.

CATHERINE PARR: My husband?

KATHERINE HOWARD: My husband, I think you'll find.

ANNE OF CLEVES: It is I who am to be married to the English könig, Henry!

JANE SEYMOUR: I fear you are mistaken. Henry is my husband.

ANNE BOLEYN: As if! He'd never go for a little mouse like you!

CATHERINE OF ARAGON: Henry has had but one wife in all his days, and I am she.

MISSY: Well, I see you six have a lot to talk about. Let's leave that for the moment. Let's talk about methods instead.

LUCRETIA BORGIA: Poison. You can be hands off, also you can poison many men with a single draught.

MISSY: Like it, Lucy!

CIRCE has joined the group.

MISSY: Hang on, who are you?

CIRCE: I am Circe the enchantress.

MISSY: I didn't invite you!

CIRCE: I am a daughter of the gods! I need no invitation! I go where I please!

MISSY: Right … and what do you think about men, then?

CIRCE: I use my magicks to enchant them and turn them into pigs.

MISSY: Pigs?

CIRCE: Yes. Look, here's an anti-men joke. 'Why can't men get mad cow disease? Because all men are pigs!'

MARIE ANTOINETTE: Qu'est-ce que le 'mad cow disease'?

CIRCE: OK, that one might have been a bit too modern. Try this one: 'How do you get a sick pig to the hospital? In a hambulance!'

MISSY: What's that got to do with men?

CIRCE: Oh, good point, I may have just moved on to general pig jokes there.

MISSY: Well, be quiet like a good girl and let me get on with my plan.

CIRCE: 'Good girl'? Isn't that a bit sexist?

MISSY: Oh, man up.

CIRCE: 'Man up'? That's a bit sexist too.

MISSY: Look, you stupid woman–

CIRCE: Sexist!

MISSY: Just grow a pair, will you?

CIRCE: Sooooooo sexist!

MISSY: Bitch.

CIRCE: Oh, now you've done it. Fellow women! Is this the person you want to help you in your struggle against an unequal world?

ELEANOR OF AQUITAINE: Thou doth say words unto us that I like not.

CALAMITY JANE: Ain't no sister of mine!

NELL GWYN: Let's go and form our own group, me ducks.

MISSY: Oh, sod off the lot of you, you ungrateful –

CIRCE: Oh, by the way, just make sure you press the little button on the back of your extra-smartphones when you go, OK? It's marked 'self-destruct memory wipe', but don't worry about that.

POPE JOAN and 16 others have left the group.

MISSY: They've all gone. Thanks for that.

CIRCE: Sorry, but you knew I'd have to foil your plan in the end.

MISSY: Really?

CIRCE: It took me a while to work out, but once I had – well, I couldn't let it go ahead, could I?

MISSY: Some might say that was just a little bit presumptuous of you.

CIRCE: I noticed you contacted a lot of people from sixteenth-century England. All of Henry VIII's wives. Lady Jane Grey and Mary Tudor – the poor Nine Day Queen and the Queen who deposed her. Mary, Queen of Scots, who lost her head when her cousin Elizabeth thought she might be plotting against her. And of course Elizabeth herself – Gloriana, the so-called Virgin Queen and, as I happen to know personally, the most significant woman of Tudor times. Now they're all very notable women, but why such a cluster? That's what I asked myself.

MISSY: Did you, poppet? Hurrah for you. And for goodness' sake (notice I said 'goodness' there, because I am now very, very good and do things for the sake of goodness), change your name. It's distracting me. I keep fancying a bacon sandwich.

Name **"DOCTOR"** is already taken.

Name **"THEDOCTOR"** is already taken.

Name **"DRJOHNSMITH"** is already taken.

Name **"DOCTORWHO"** is already taken.

Name **"DOCTOR12"** is already taken.

Name **"DOCTOR???"** is already taken.

Name **"DRDISCO"** is already taken.

Name **"DRMYSTERIO"** is already taken.

Name **"OHTHISISRIDICULOUS"** is already taken.

Name **"THATWASN'TASUGGESTIONYOU STUPIDPIECEOFJUNK"** is still available!

Change name?

CIRCE: You'll just have to put up with this one. I coped with all the Emil Keller / Kalid / Professor Yana stuff over the years.

MISSY: Oh, we did have a laugh, didn't we?

CIRCE: I don't remember laughing much.

MISSY: I did, though. Your face! I lived for that moment. Off with the wig and – Ha! The way your jaw dropped. I mean, I knew that sometimes you already knew it was me and you were just doing the face to please me. That was so sweet of you.

CIRCE: I am not sweet.

MISSY: Don't be silly. All the times I could just eat you up! Crunch you with your celery! Actually, I have a theory about you and jelly babies, I'll have to tell you about it some time.

CIRCE: ANYWAY. I was about to expose your plan.

MISSY: Yes, you were, weren't you. I was looking forward to hearing what it was.

CIRCE: There had to be a reason why you included nearly all the Tudor women in your little gang. Some of them, after all, didn't need your advice. Mary and Elizabeth were already female rulers in a man's world. Then I thought about what came after the Tudors. The very next ruler after Elizabeth was James I. And do you know what James I did? He granted Royal Charters for various organisations – such as universities. One of those universities included the institution that later became St Luke's – the very place where you are now incarcerated. So. No James I – no charter – no university – no St Luke's – no vault. You were throwing stones into the Tudor puddle and hoping the Stuart dynasty splashed out of existence. Almost anything could have done it – one of the wives bumping off Henry, Bloody Mary burning a few more men here or there, James's mum getting rid of Darnley before they'd done the dirty, Elizabeth deciding she wasn't going to let some Scottish boy take over her throne. Only one of those things had to happen, and you'd go free. But you knew I'd be watching you.

MISSY: Well, most of the time it's been the little hobgoblin with glasses, but yes, carry on.

CIRCE: You were clever, I'll give you that. You did it in an openly sneaky way.

MISSY: Well, wasn't I the clever-clogs. What does that mean exactly?

CIRCE: You asked for the components to make a space-time telegraph, slipping them in among other deliberately chosen bizarre requests so it wouldn't seem blatant, but knowing I'd spot you. Which I did, long before Nardole, I'd like to point out for the record. Then you began your supposedly secret operation, again knowing I'd be fully aware of what you were doing. You were banking on me being so pleased I'd caught you out that I'd never spot what you were really up to. All the other historical women – Boudicca, Marie Curie, Helen of Troy – they were just window-dressing. Your first, last, and only goal was to prevent James I taking the throne of England so you could escape captivity.

MISSY: Oh, brilliant. Quite, quite brilliant. One of those little applauding hands pictures.

CIRCE: You forget how well I know you.

MISSY: Yes, oh yes! Oh Doctor, you know me better than I know myself! I fall at your feet in humble admiration! I have been caught out! My plan has been exposed! You are the biggest brainbox in the whole of Fairyland. I throw myself at your feet in supplication.

CIRCE: All right, there's no need for all of that.

MISSY: But how can I resist when your giant brain is making me go all gooey and girlie?

CIRCE: Look, we'll take apart the space-time telegraph and say no more about it.

MISSY: But I want to say some more! I want to say how your giant brain must be encased inside a BIG HEAD!

CIRCE: What?

MISSY: So full of yourself! And so full of doggy doo-doo. All that just to stop a university being built? There are a hundred easier ways I could have sorted that, and you wouldn't have known a thing about it. But what difference would it have made anyway? You'd just have built this silly vault somewhere else. Plus – you know, I did agree to this. Obviously I'm not enjoying it. But if I really wanted to get out – *really* – then I'd be out. I think you know that deep in your little hearts.

CIRCE: So if that wasn't your plan – what were you doing?

MISSY: My plan was exactly what I said it was. To help women.

CIRCE: In order to disrupt history.

MISSY: In order to make things better!

CIRCE: What, really?

MISSY: Yes, really! Look, I did a wee bit of reading, and it turns out that for most of the history of this planet, men have treated women a teensy bit badly. As a woman, I object to that, so I decided to help. I didn't try to keep it secret from you, not even a little bit. Because I thought you'd *approve*!

CIRCE: You thought I'd approve of you telling women to stab men and turn their insides into spaghetti!

MISSY: YES! Telling them to turn on their oppressors! Isn't that what you always do? I was trying to be like you!

MISSY: Are you still there?

MISSY: You've gone all quiet.

MISSY: Shall I sing a song to pass the time? Any requests? I do a mean Lulu impression. *We-e-eee-ee-ee-elll –*

CIRCE: You're saying that not only did you feel empathy for certain humans, you wanted to help them, and you wanted to be like me?

MISSY: No, I didn't say any of that.

CIRCE: You did, it's still there on the screen.

MISSY: I was lying. It was the James I thing really.

CIRCE: I think, in your own way, you really were trying to do a good thing. You are changing.

MISSY: Wash that sassy mouth out! I just wanted some historical ladies to get all stabby-stabby on King James, then whoops! I'm out of the Vault, bye-bye Doctor and little bald hobgoblin man.

CIRCE: You wanted to right an injustice.

MISSY: Will you stop saying that! You're giving me a headache. Anyway, my plan failed. Whichever one it was. Still stuck in the Vault, human history still rubbish to women.

CIRCE: There are other ways you can help get them justice.

MISSY: Not bleedin' likely, guv'nor. Ungrateful lot! Throwing all my brilliant ideas back in my face! I'm 100% done with human women. Hate the lot of them. Hope they all use lead-based make-up and die. Next time I'll pick someone else to help.

CIRCE: Aha!

MISSY: Not that I'm saying there'll be a next time. Or that I was trying to help anyone in the first place.

CIRCE: So why were there so many Tudors on your list?

MISSY: Just because I read a good book on them. Books are good. You should read a book sometimes. You might learn something. Plus there was a *lot* of burning and beheading. Enough to make any girl's hearts flutter. Anyway, nice talking to you, Doctor. I have to go now, the hobgoblin has brought me a cup of tea and I need to dunk things in it.

MISSY has left the conversation.

*

Dear Doctor,

These are the things she's asked for this week:

1 x pair of time tweezers.

A book on what intelligent species there are on this idiotic planet apart from humans.

1 x pack of chocolate garrottes.

Yours sincerely,
Nardole

N. Book is OK. I don't think chocolate garrottes are a real thing. And what on Earth are time tweezers? D

D. Apparently if you pluck your eyebrows, they regrow backwards in time so you never have to do it again, but your past self might get a hairy chin or something ohhhhhh.

*

Your Andromeda.gal.ax order #ZZ9-ZZZ-F
Delivery Update

Hello Mr N A Rdole!
We're going to deliver your package today.

Delivery Information:
'Intelligent Life on Earth: Real or Myth?' (jellyback) by X'c'zzEvnh.

This is the final part of your order. Your order is now complete.

*

INVITATION

Dear Rattus rattus 1
You are invited to join RAT (Rodents Against Terrans).

I can't be doing with apes, they're basically just extra-hairy humans, and I'm totally off the sea following a bad experience with some reptiles in the 1970s (or was it the 1980s?) so the dolphins are out too, which means the rats have won the lottery! You're pretty much as intelligent as humans but do they treat you like you are? No! Rat traps! Rat poison! Lab rats! Rat baiting! Flushing you down the loo! Now, there's at least one rat for every human on Earth, you can reproduce at a frankly embarrassing rate and your teeth grow five inches in a year, so things are stacked in your favour. You had a good try with plagues back in the day, but it's time to take things to a new level. RATS RULE!

RSVP

Your friend,
Missy

Alit in Underland
Richard Dinnick

The scarecrows were mumbling again. They did that from time to time. It was one of the weird things about coming to the homestead. The eerie muttering did not bother the two people Alit was following. She had seen them arguing with Hazran and the other new arrival – the funny bald man, Nardole. She often hid in the shadows and secretly listened to what the grown-ups were talking about. Mostly it was just boring stuff, but this time it was quite good.

Alit loved exploring and finding stuff out. She always had. To do that, though, meant she didn't always do as she was told or stay this side of the fence. As far as she was concerned, you could only find out how far you could go by going too far. At least that's what her mum had always told her. So she was good at hiding in shadows and around corners, eavesdropping and watching. Adults didn't really notice children, and even if they did, they assumed that being small meant they couldn't understand what was going on.

Alit had a pretty good idea.

The bearded man who called himself the Master told Hazran that he planned to go down to Floor 508 to see if there was a way to stop the scarecrows and whoever was making them … to escape from something he called the Exodus. His friend, or girlfriend, or whoever she was – the woman called Missy – said she would go with him.

Alit was interested in the woman. She had the craziest hair the little girl had ever seen. She acted kind of nice but also a bit scary, too. Like she almost had a heart but not quite. The Master, on the other hand, was an odd and frightening man – all nasty comments and exaggerated gestures. Hazran had already told the children to stay out of his way because, she said, he was a cowardly bully.

Nardole said he didn't think going back down to the lower levels was a good idea and that they should wait for the Doctor to wake up.

'You might need to ask permission before you do something,' the Master said. 'I do not.'

'Nor do I,' Alit breathed softly. 'And I'm going to keep an eye on you.'

Everyone knew you shouldn't go out at night. That was when the scarecrows came. Hazran made the children hide under their beds while the grown-ups went out with guns and shot at the scarecrows. But not tonight.

*

As Missy and the Master made their way across the nocturnal landscape of greys and blues, there was nothing to disturb their progress and Alit followed them easily – the holographic moon above giving just enough light by which to see.

Whatever the Master was hoping to find, something told Alit he wasn't going to share it with anyone but Missy. And if it could help, if it could stop the scarecrows, somehow, or in their escape …

'Escape,' she breathed. Alit loved the sound of the word like she loved the feeling of breaking the rules. It was why she'd been sent to Hazran in the first place: to be kept under someone's eye for her own safety. But Alit was just as good at sneaking out of the house undetected as she was at following people.

The Master and Missy were deep in conversation and didn't notice Alit as she trailed them through the woods. Every now and again, one of them would turn round and gaze into the semi-darkness. Alit would hide behind a tree or lie flat on the ground, trying to control her breathing – half excited and half scared.

Alit could hear them as they neared the hole the spaceship had made when it crashed through the floor. The place where she'd first met them. She now scooted round behind them so that she was hiding behind the wreck of the shuttlecraft the strangers had arrived in. Alit peered around the corner of the ship at the two grown-ups. They were staring into the metallic hole the ship had made when it erupted through the floor.

The Master was shining what Alit took to be a torch into the crater. 'There!' He pointed with his other hand. 'Superstructure walkways between the ceiling of the level below and the ground of the level above.'

'Oh, yes!' Missy sounded impressed. 'Clever. Probably used for holo-emitter access and maintenance.'

'I agree,' the bearded man replied. 'But then, I would, wouldn't I?'

Soon Missy had fetched the metal rope ladder from the downed shuttle and was spooling it over the edge of the crater. When it was fully extended, Missy started the precarious climb down into the maw of darkness the shuttle had created, and the Master followed.

Once they had both disappeared from view, Alit slipped from the side of the ship and eased forward to crane her neck over the crater. She couldn't see them, but she could still hear them – bickering with one another. It was clear they were both crazy, and even an adventurous soul like Alit knew when she should quit and head for home. But then she turned around and saw it standing there.

A scarecrow.

Like the others that the grown-ups placed on crosspieces during the day, it was dressed from top to toe in silver with an eyeless stocking over its head and two tubes feeding some form of liquid into holes where the nostrils should be. It was also all crooked and hunched; its head to one side like it was listening to something very faint. And even though it had no eyes, Alit could feel it *looking* at her. Alit's own eyes widened in fear, and she almost let out a little scream. She managed to stifle it, aware that the Master and Missy were somewhere below her on the ladder.

The ladder! Alit turned and saw it dangling in the darkness. Could scarecrows climb? If they could, she guessed, they would be *really* slow. It was her only chance.

Just as the ghostlike figure of the scarecrow was almost upon her, Alit launched herself away from it, grabbing for the safety of the ladder. She managed to catch one of the rungs with both hands and caused the ladder to swing and twist.

'Oi!' came a manly voice from below.

'Wheeeee,' the unmistakeable voice of Missy joined in, sounding like a child on a swing.

Alit quickly climbed down and found the two grown-ups staring at her as if she were a bug in their jam. They were standing on a metal floor belonging to a corridor that had been severed by the shuttle when it had blasted through the floor. It continued on the other side of the crater, receding into darkness. The Master was pointing his torch device at her, but it was not lit.

'Who are you?' he asked, frowning.

'You don't need your laser screwdriver!' Missy said. 'She's from the homestead. Alit, wasn't it?' She moved forward and plucked Alit from the ladder before plonking her unceremoniously on the floor. Then she squatted and examined Alit's face. 'My question would be: why did you follow us down here?' Missy smiled a very unconvincing smile.

'The scarecrow!' Alit said and pointed back up the ladder. She certainly wasn't going to tell them the truth: that she didn't trust them and wanted to know what they were doing.

'Scarecrow?' the Master asked. 'You mean the partially converted Cyberman?'

Alit was confused and couldn't hide it on her face, wrinkling her nose and knotting her brows.

Missy sighed. 'Of course she does. But she doesn't know what a Cyberman is, do you?'

Alit shook her head.

'Not yet, anyway,' the Master said with some relish. 'Let it catch her. She'll find out. The scarecrow will get himself a brain ...'

'And boost the Cybermen's numbers?' Missy rose and gave an exaggerated nod. 'Just what we want. Besides, Alit looks useful. Small. Agile.' She stood up again, levelling her umbrella down the dimly lit walkway. 'Shall we go this way?'

The Master turned on his heel and began to walk in the opposite direction. 'No,' he said. 'This way.'

Alit looked up at Missy, wondering how the woman would take this defiance from her friend.

'You're probably a wee bit scared now, aren't you?' Missy asked in a whisper. 'The scarecrow? The dark? Even Mr Grumpy-Beard there!' She waved her brolly at the receding back of the Master. 'S'OK, though. I promise!' Missy took the little girl's hand in hers and squeezed just a little too tightly. 'There's only one thing you should be scared of around here and it isn't any of *them*!'

The space between floors was only just tall enough for the grown-ups to walk without banging their heads. This access space was made up of straight corridors with endless junctions. The walls were completely smooth other than where there were control panels or monitoring stations and these were pretty few and far between. Each time they found one, the group would stop so the Master and Missy could make an examination.

Alit was fascinated by all this. Both of them had such a sense of purpose, such confidence in what they were doing. As if nothing could really harm them. Alit wished she was like them, but every now and again doubt would sweep through her, nagging at her that she should be back in bed, let other people worry about this. But she'd seen that scarecrow up close, seen the relentless way of it. Alit knew that nowhere was safe now.

The Master speculated that there must be some kind of service lift: an elevator that only served the access space and the level below. They started to search for it. However, every time they thought they'd found it, it would turn out to be an auxiliary generator or a holo-emitter relay or some other piece of equipment. Anything but a lift.

Strip-lights provided some dull illumination. This world of tight, narrow corridors, burnished metal and constant twilight was very much an alien one to Alit. Her home was one of green fields and cosy farm buildings, barns and windmills, however artificial. But now she knew what lay beneath it: a dark and shadowy world with weird, distant noises and the threat of the unknown around every corner.

Alit kept thinking she'd seen the scarecrow, the one Missy had taken to calling 'Topknot'. It was just a shape in the semi-darkness – a long way off – but Alit was sure she'd seen it move. To make things worse, all of them had heard a clattering sound, not long ago now, that could only have been someone knocking something over – someone clumsy or lumbering …

They had picked up the pace after that. They had just walked past another four-way junction in the corridors when Missy paused mid-step. She was examining the handle of her umbrella.

The Master noticed this and turned back to her with some annoyance. 'Well?' he said.

'I think there's a service cradle here,' she said, moving down the right-hand corridor until she stood beside a large metal hatch that was firmly shut. 'Like a platform used for cleaning the windows on tall buildings.'

The Master came alongside Missy and looked at her through narrowed eyes. 'I've been meaning to ask you about that,' the Master said, waving an appalled hand at Missy's umbrella. 'That and the hat you were wearing before. It's all a bit …'

'What?'

'Well. A bit … Mary Poppins.'

'Oh, you know we've always had a bit of a *penchant* for children's viewing.'

'When we came here, I expected that big, baby sun to rise over the meadows.' The Master laughed. 'And remember those pink things? The knitted ones that went "hoo-hoo-hoo-hoo" when they talked.'

'*The Clangers,*' Missy said.

Alit looked between them, not understanding the conversation but sensing undercurrents beneath it.

'I've been watching a lot of children's films recently.' Missy fiddled with her umbrella and it made a whirring sound. 'We watched *Frozen* together.'

'We?'

Missy shot the Master a guilty, apologetic look from under her eyelashes.

The Master turned away in disgust. 'Was he torturing you?'

Missy frowned. 'This door is deadlock sealed,' she said.

The Master folded his arms and shook his head. 'No, no, no. You don't get off that easily. I can't believe you watched *Frozen* – **Frozen**! – with the Doctor!'

Missy looked at him, a twinkle in her eye. 'Let it go,' she said.

The Master turned his attention to the metal hatch. 'Deadlock sealed? Lucky I have a laser screwdriver, then.' He glanced at Missy's umbrella with another brief shake of his head. 'Who'd have sonic?' He quickly set to work, cutting through the hatch seals with the torch-like device. When he'd finished, he stood back theatrically and the door fell to the floor with a resounding clang. 'Ta-da!'

Without warning, the scarecrow lunged from the shadows and snatched at Missy. She saw it at the last second and ducked away, blocking its grabbing hand with the handle of her umbrella. Alit dived through the open hatchway.

'Oh, no, you don't!' The Master was already moving, snatching at the cloth that covered the Cyberman's chest. He ripped it open to reveal a computerised display unit beneath. The Cyberman tried to grab at his assailant, but Missy was parrying his movements with her umbrella, accompanying each move with a squeal of '*Hai!*'

The Master stared at the chest unit for a brief second, then used his laser screwdriver to make a fine incision. Immediately the Cyberman stopped flailing and stood still. 'There!' The Master stood back, a little out of breath.

Missy sank to the floor and looked up at the inert Cyberman. 'What have you done to poor Topknot?'

'Downgraded it,' the Master replied. 'Now, let's see what it has to say for itself.' He stepped up to the Cyberman and looked it in the face before lowering his head to the top of the chest unit. 'Voice box, voice box …' He fiddled with some unseen controls then stood back.

'Pain,' the Cyberman said. 'Pain.'

'I agree,' the Master said. 'In the backside.'

Alit poked her head from the hatch, shivering, to check it was safe once more.

The Master spoke to the Cyberman again. 'Recognise vocal command authorisation: Master. Alpha. Seven,' he said.

'You perfected voice control?' Missy breathed. 'Impressive!'

'What did you expect?' The Master unbuttoned the back of the Cyberman's silver overall and explained that he was going to change the root command in its operating system so that it no longer identified beings with two hearts as a target. 'Then we can use Topknot here for whatever we like. He has scanning capability and he's strong.'

While the Master worked, Missy went to look at the service cradle. It was approximately two metres wide by four metres long and looked like a cage, with thick strips of metal wrapped around the superstructure roughly a quarter of a metre apart. Although the Master had burnt away the door to the space in which the cradle was housed, the platform itself was still locked.

Missy looked at Alit and smiled. 'Oh, look. You're just small enough to squeeze in there.'

Alit was still staring at the scarecrow, unnerved by its presence but glad to see it under control – even if the person controlling it was the Master. She turned to Missy and bobbed her head. 'Easy,' she said.

Alit pushed herself between the bars and quickly unlocked the door. She stepped through the opening, striking a dramatic pose as she did so. 'Ta-da!' she mimicked the Master's earlier cry. Missy laughed and clapped her hands together.

The Master appeared in the doorway again. 'What's going on?' he asked.

'I think we have a protégé,' Missy replied.

'You might have a protégé, but I have a slave.' He stepped aside to reveal the scarecrow standing obediently behind him. 'Take us down.'

Topknot walked over to the controls and, after a brief moment analysing their functions, operated one of them with its rubber-gloved hand.

With a hydraulic growl, the doors beneath the service cradle opened and immediately the passengers within could feel a strong wind ruffling their clothes and blowing against their faces. More clanking noises indicated the winches coming online, and the platform jerked away from its housing and down into the sky of Floor 508. It was still night-time down there, and the firmament was an inky blue with nothing to see below save indistinct blackness.

'Welcome to "Underland"!' Missy called above the roar of the wind.

The Master slid down the bench so he was pressed up against his female alter ego. 'Why are you so chipper?' he hissed.

'Aren't we always?'

'No!' He seemed to have a bad taste in his mouth and looked her up and down. 'I think it's to do with our latest regeneration.'

'You're not very keen on becoming a woman, are you?'

'Girls have a way of … disappointing you. One minute they're all lovey-dovey and the next they stab you in the back! They're so … *fickle.*'

'Hasn't stopped us using women in the past, has it?'

'I use everyone.'

'Galleia, Kassia, Chantho, Miss Trefusis.'

'You remember the names. How sweet.' He pursed his lips, pouting at Missy.

'I've been making myself recall them recently, yes.' Missy allowed herself a brief smile of resignation. 'Lucy, of course.'

'And you're using a child!' the Master added. 'Alit! Oh, Alit!' He called the little girl over to them.

Reluctantly, Alit tore her attention away from staring over the side of the cradle and moved over to stand in front of the two grown-ups.

'Do you have a mummy? A daddy?' the Master asked.

Alit nodded. 'They said I had to come to the farmstead.'

'An evacuee,' Missy said.

'And do you like any of the boys there?'

'Or girls,' Missy added. 'Isn't that the right thing to say?'

Alit looked at her feet. 'Omebo's OK,' she mumbled.

'And if you married Omebo—'

'I'm not going to marry him!'

'Never interrupt me.' The Master's eyes had narrowed and his voice was dangerous and quiet. 'If you married Omebo, little Alit, you wouldn't betray him, would you?'

Alit shook her head.

'Of course you wouldn't,' the Master said sarcastically. 'Just like Chantho and lovely Lucy Saxon.'

'Lucy wanted a way out,' Missy said with a note of irony in her voice. 'And that almost cost you everything, didn't it?'

'Like I say: fickle.'

Missy looked away for a moment as if she found something painful. 'So what's the plan? That rubbish you spouted for Nardole might have fooled him, but it didn't wash with me. "Stop the Cybermen, find an escape." Really?' Her eyes darted to Alit, who simply stared back at her, as if she didn't understand. She was good at that look. She'd practised it in front of the mirror sometimes.

The Master grinned. 'The Doctor has taken away our chance to lead an army, to subjugate and dominate the galaxy. Well, not any more. I'm going to change that one digit the Doctor altered when we were on Floor 1056 – the number of hearts the Cybermen identify as human – from a "two" back to a "one".' He leaned forward and cupped his hand over Missy's ear, eyeing Alit suspiciously. 'I regain control of the Cybermen. Of everyone!'

'Exciting!' Missy breathed.

'Why are you whispering?' Alit was looking directly at them. 'What are you even talking about – control everyone?'

'Just silly grown-up stuff,' Missy said.

Yeah, right. Alit decided it was best to act dumb. 'Where are we going anyway? Can't you use Topknot to help us now? Why do we need to use this cradle thing?'

The Master leant forward, very earnestly, his hands clasped together. His voice was very calm and measured. 'Can I ask you a question?'

'All right,' Alit said uneasily.

The Master blew out a weary breath and whined: 'Are we there yet?'

The ground was only thirty metres away now. Even in the weak dawn light, Alit could tell it was an amazing yellowy-gold colour and stretched for a long way in every direction. It bordered several other huge fields each a slightly different colour indicating a different crop.

The cradle bumped onto the ground just as the artificial sun came up, sending rays of peachy light across the huge expanse of corn and illuminating a grid of bronzed pathways that criss-crossed the patchwork of fields.

They had landed on a small square of concrete adjacent to a much larger circular area where two of the bronze paths crossed one another. Now they were close to them, they could see these paths were slightly raised off the ground, about two metres wide with a channel running down the middle.

The Master was already off the platform and examining one of them. 'It's a rail of some kind,' he reported. 'The central groove is for guidance. Maybe a power feed within?' He tapped the wide, flat metal. 'Whatever rides them is big.'

As he finished speaking, the ground began to vibrate with a low rumble and they all turned towards the source of the noise. Coming down along the flattened rail was a huge machine. It was as big as the farmstead Alit had recently moved to and was bearing down on them at speed.

The Master stood and retreated back to the square area and leant against the side of the maintenance cradle. Topknot was still standing beside the platform next to Missy and Alit.

'Some form of automated harvester for the crops,' the Master said. 'We'll let it pass and then follow it.'

'Why?' asked Alit.

The Master mimicked her mouth with his hand and a sarcastic expression flashed across his face. 'Because, *little girl*, that's the only technology here, and wherever it's taking the corn is where we'll find more – technology we can actually use.'

They had to wait as the machine came to a halt alongside them, reaching the crossroads in its guidance rail. It turned slowly in a ninety-degree arc. As it did so, Alit could see it was a featureless block of metal with various hatches and control access panels along its front and sides. There was no room for a driver let alone passengers.

A hatch that ran the length of the front of the machine opened and a huge churning drum of blades appeared. The robo-tractor then set off across the field, the drum rotating and chopping the corn down.

As the wheat was harvested at the front, further attachments scooped the straw down a separate tube, clearly using a vacuum to suck it up and make sure nothing was lost. Two further flaps had opened at the rear of the vehicle and multi-headed ploughs were extending from them, churning the stubble left behind back into the rich, dark earth. The bronze path now positively glowed a rich, deep yellow in the light from the fully risen sun.

'Shall we?' the Master said, indicating they should start following it.

He waited for Missy to join him, and she slipped her arm through his. Then she grabbed Alit's hand and together with the scarecrow the four of them began walking briskly up the yellowy road.

It became evident that while Missy and the Master could walk at a steady pace for what seemed like an eternity, Alit could not. She had been slowing for the last twenty minutes, and the Master was not helping matters by sighing and making sarcastic remarks. Missy had suggested that Topknot carry the little girl, but Alit had refused stubbornly. Fortunately, they were all saved by the arrival of a second type of vehicle on the bronzed railroad.

This one was lower and less square; it had a small front section with a much larger rear section – like a bloated spider. This mechanical arachnid did not have eight legs, however, just the one. It was massively long and wide, and stretched over a hundred metres into the field beside the track. Its job seemed to be to plant new seeds and to administer some form of growth accelerant. The moment its arm passed over the ground, a green shoot appeared, poking up from the nutrient-infused earth.

The fact that this cultivator machine was squatter also meant that the four unlikely travellers could board it by climbing onto its back. They had to run to do so. Alit climbed on easily. Missy had a bit more difficulty and the little girl had to help her, pulling her up with the aid of the woman's umbrella. Soon they were all riding the machine, happy to sit in the artificial sunshine and gaze up at the faint numbers that denoted the floor number projected onto the ceiling high above.

Once aboard the cultivator, it did not take them long to leave the corn fields behind and enter a very different expanse. It was approaching dusk as they made their approach via an area of stubby plants with broad leaves. Alit took pleasure in naming the different crops as they passed, eager to show off her knowledge.

'Potatoes!' she cried.

'*Solanum tuberosum*,' the Master said through a yawn.

Alit snorted. 'No, they're definitely potatoes.'

'They don't have Latin on Mondas,' Missy drawled.

'This isn't Mondas,' the Master replied, folding his arms. He was soon on his feet, though, and happy to see what now lay ahead of them: a vast swathe of the landscape on the horizon was given over to dark green towers of differing heights that soared into the sky. As they neared them, it became clear the towers were actually silos for the storage of the very crops that surrounded them.

'Do you think these crops were for a native human population?' Missy asked, staring out at the fields. 'Or do you think there is some automated delivery system for the floors above?'

'A bit of both, I should think.' The Master stroked his beard, thinking. 'Alit, where do you get your potatoes from? Most of the land around the farmstead is pasture and woodland for livestock.'

'The carters bring them,' Alit said. 'And hay and straw. When I was really little, they used to come all the time, but not so much now.'

'A delivery system, then,' Missy said. 'Interesting ...'

Finally, fields no longer flanked the bronzed railroad. Instead, warehouses of various sizes took their place. The cultivator accelerated, and the Master said they should get ready to disembark. Sure enough the track split into many different branch lines that led to assorted warehouses and garages.

Just as the cultivator slowed to make its turning, the Master slid to the ground and held his hand out for Missy to follow. Instead she jumped into the air floating slowly back to the ground using her umbrella in an impossible way to slow her descent. Alit couldn't help but smile at this while the Master just shook his head. Alit slid off the side of the vehicle, but landed awkwardly, ripping the sole of her slipper in the process.

It only occurred to her then that she wasn't dressed for adventuring. As if copying her, Topknot stumbled from the cultivator and fell to the floor, his leg twisted at a nasty angle under him. Alit went cautiously over to help but the Master brushed her away and yanked the scarecrow to its feet. No soothing murmurs, no hugs. Alit supposed the scarecrow was in too much pain to notice much more.

'Right,' the Master said. 'We need to find the heart of the operation.'

Missy nodded to Topknot. 'Better ask the Tin Man.'

The Master smiled humourlessly and then asked the Cyberman to scan for technology they could use to access the ship's systems. 'Once we do that,' he said to Missy, 'we can hack into the ones I set up on Floor 1056.'

Topknot turned in a circle and then lifted an arm towards a tower at the centre of the surrounding buildings. 'There.'

Although the outskirts of the agricultural metropolis had been made up of individual structures, those ahead of them in the centre were all part of one giant edifice, almost like a bucolic cathedral with soaring grain silos for bell towers, domed tractor garages for galleries and elongated warehouses for naves.

Just as the sun was setting for the day, Missy used her umbrella to gain access to the nearest building. The Master used Topknot like a homing device to guide them through the various chambers. It was while they were making their way through a darkened warehouse that they first heard the others.

The Master was examining a pile of shovels on a vast shelf. 'Looks like they have all sorts of equipment here – even ones for people to use.'

'There are gumboots over there!' Alit called, racing off and pulling boot after boot from the shelves until she found a pair that fitted her.

'You *shall* go to the ball!' Missy said.

'What are you two *doing*?' the Master shouted over to them.

'Shoe shopping!' Missy called back. 'It's a girly girl thing, probably. You wouldn't understand!'

Their raised voices were echoing down the aisles when they heard something echo back to them.

'Leader. Target detected! Two-hearts . . .'

'*Excellent.*'

Missy immediately ducked down to hide. She pulled Alit down with her and beckoned to the Master, placing one finger on her lips. Topknot remained immobile, safely hidden from view as if the Master had told it to 'stay'.

'Did you hear what it said?' the Master hissed. 'They're specifically looking for two-hearts.' He smiled. 'They're looking for *us.*'

Before Missy could react, the Master was on his feet and walking briskly towards the source of the Cyber-voices. Missy followed him. So did Alit, albeit reluctantly.

They rounded a corner and came face to face with a group of six Cybermen. Alit stopped in her tracks, very scared now. These were significantly more advanced than Topknot and the other scarecrows. Instead of the cumbersome chest units and limb supports, these ones wore something like padded silver overalls with a raised plate on their chests housing a small grille. Their helmets were more complex yet more streamlined with simpler 'handles' and an angled bridge across where their noses should be.

One of the Cybermen had black handles. It moved forward and stood towering over the Master.

'We meet again,' it intoned.

'Really? I'm not sure.' The Master scratched his beard as if trying to recollect a prior encounter.

'Your form is known to us,' one of the other Cybermen replied. It was closest to the leader, acting as his deputy or lieutenant.

'You are the Master,' added the black-handled one. 'The former ruler of our world.'

'Very good,' the Master said, smiling. 'So why are you here?'

'Leader! Questions from humans have no validity!'

'This one is not human,' the Cyber-Leader said. 'We are a pathfinder group. We have been sent to find you.' It gave an inclusive wave of its right hand. '*Both* of you.'

'Both?'

'The two-hearts. The small female is of no consequence. She will be converted when we return to Floor 1056.'

Alit hid behind Missy.

'What are your orders, then? What's our … *fate*?' the Master asked.

'The Cyber-Planner orders interrogation and further study.'

'Cyber-Planner? Interesting.' The Master stepped up to the Leader and held out his hands in supplication. 'In that case, I am the Master and your humble servant.'

Missy frowned. 'Really? Again? You know where this ends – on a draughty kitchen floor …'

The Leader moved forward, threateningly. 'Enough.'

'Why does the Cyber-Planner want to interrogate us?' Missy said quickly. 'Why not simply upgrade us?'

'The Cyber-Planner has noted that our programmed definition of humanity has been altered. Such tampering constitutes a threat to our autonomy. We require to know why and how the change was made – and who made it – in order to prevent its recurrence.' The Cyber-Leader unshouldered a blunt-looking weapon and levelled it at the trio before him. The other Cybermen followed suit. 'Now. You will accompany us.'

'Return to Floor 1056?' the Master asked as he turned around and walked ahead of the Cybermen.

'Yes. The lifts will take us back to the Cyber factories.'

'The lifts. Aha!' The Master smiled at Missy. 'Could save a lot of time.'

They walked in silence for a few minutes until they reached a set of three lift doors. Beside it was the entrance to a storage cupboard. A Cyberman stood guard beside it.

'What's that?' Missy asked.

'You are to be held here until we can descend.'

'Why?' Missy frowned.

The Master, however, was smiling and pointing his finger at the Cyber-Leader.

'Ooh. He's got other orders, haven't you?' the Master asked, one eyebrow arched. 'What is it, then. A secondary mission?'

'Our orders do not concern you,' the Cyber-Leader said. 'Place them in the cell.'

Two Cybermen moved forward but the Master turned to Missy and nodded. 'Now!'

Missy raised her umbrella and, before the Cybermen could open fire, it emitted a horrible, high-pitched warbling. The Cybermen began to shake. The Master snatched his laser screwdriver from his pocket and fired it at the Cyber-Lieutenant's chest plate. Sparks exploded from the grille there.

Alit screamed, and Missy yanked the girl by the arm and started running, disappearing down a side corridor – and from view. They took refuge in a small closet set into the wall. Alit peered under the door, her heart pounding in her chest.

The Cyber-Leader had grabbed the Master from behind, crushing his chest with punishing force, and hurled him, unconscious, into the cell.

The other Cybermen had formed a defensive pattern around the lifts, weapons raised.

The Leader then turned to the nearest two Cybermen. 'You will find the woman and the child.'

'Yes, Leader.' They began marching towards Alit and Missy's hiding place.

'The Cybermats must be primed and released before we return to Floor 1056,' the Cyber-Leader ordered.

Two further Cybermen threw their arms across their chests in salute and moved off, turning left down one of the side walkways.

Alit tugged at Missy's skirt as the Cybermen came nearer. Missy nodded and pointed to the back of the closet. Alit frowned but watched as Missy silently moved to the far wall and opened it, showing another corridor beyond. The wall was double sided.

Missy snatched Alit's hand and started tiptoeing briskly away. 'Cybermats?' she whispered to herself. 'That is interesting.'

'What's a Cybermat?' Alit asked. She was sitting on a chair high up in the control tower they had seen earlier, swinging her legs to and fro as they didn't quite touch the ground.

Missy was sitting on the floor, surrounded by wires and ducting that she had pulled from service hatches in the control room's walls. She was biting her lip, concentrating as she used her umbrella to influence the controls and alter the holographic display projected in front of her.

'Cybermats are like metal rats – or mice,' Missy explained, pointing at the small cage Alit now wore around her neck.

When they'd left the Cybermen back at the lifts, Missy had led them on a very erratic route to the control tower, diverting via a grain store.

'Do you know what rodents are? Do you have them on your level?'

'They get into the barns sometimes. I heard Hazran say she thought they came from the laboratory levels.'

In the grain store, Missy had quickly found and stunned a handful of mice that were feeding there, constructing small cages for the animals from fence wire. They were both now wearing the mouse cages around their necks like oversized pendants. Alit had two of them while Missy had only one.

Alit had been confused by this bizarre detour until Missy explained that it wouldn't take the Cybermen long to repair their scanners, and they were searching for targets with either one heart or two. With the mice in such close proximity to their bodies, the cyber-sensors would be fooled into grouping three heartbeats together, which meant that, logically, Alit and Missy could not be their targets and would, with any luck, be ignored.

'I doubt it'll fool them for long,' she added dourly, 'and it certainly won't fool more developed Cybermen. They'll be along soon enough.'

'And these Cybermats they have will get into the homestead and make Hazran and the others sick?'

'That's right. The Cybermen use them to spread disease to weaken human colonies so they can invade more easily.' Missy was now gazing at the projection in the control room, tinkering with some of the controls that lay strewn around her on the floor.

'Can we stop them?'

'*We* can't.'

Alit sighed and gave her mice some grains of corn she'd been carrying in her pocket. Missy had named them Hunca Munca and Tom Thumb. When Alit had asked why, the Time Lord had started telling her *The Tale of Two Bad Mice* by someone called Beatrix Potter.

By the time Missy had finished the story, they had found Topknot. Missy had ordered him to follow and she had used him both to scan for nearby Cybermen and to locate the control tower.

They'd left the scarecrow guarding the entrance on the ground floor while they had taken a lift up to the top of the tower. The view was quite spectacular, and an electronic map of the whole area was displayed on the wall. Missy had soon discovered that the main reason for the map was that the floor had an artificial weather system and this was the hub.

'That gives me a wonderful idea,' she'd said, shooting a grin and a sideways glance at Alit as she began playing the keys on the console. 'I hope you like surprises. Just hacking into the ship's computer system, getting myself access all areas. Obviously, *that's* not the surprise, I could do that in my ...' Her fingers stopped moving. 'Aha! It seems that everything old me made in that hospital had a failsafe system. I suppose to stop the patients from wandering off mid-conversion.'

Alit frowned. She didn't understand a word of what Missy had just said. 'Fail save?'

'Like a dog on a chain,' Missy elaborated. 'If they got too far from the hospital or, I suppose, the factories, their systems would yank them back. If they didn't return, the system would malfunction or shut down. In order for the Cybermen to leave Floor 1056 – for Operation Exodus to take place – that system had to be switched off. And predictably – logically – the Cybermats have the same cybernetic systems built into them.' She smiled. 'I've just found that "switch" in their programming and deadlocked it back to the original setting. Ta-da! No more nasty, bitey Cybermats on the loose!'

'Then, Hazran and the others are safe!'

'From Cybermats at least.' Missy then froze for a moment before her eyes started darting this way and that. 'Of course! If I can do that for the Cybermats, with a little help I might just be able to do it for … ooh. That's good!' She turned to the wall, whispering to herself. 'He *will* be pleased with me. Just wait till I tell him! *If* I tell him. It will be a surprise!' She laughed long and hard at this. 'Yes. A lovely surprise!'

Alit stared up at her apprehensively. 'You all right?'

'We're *all* all right!' Missy sailed across the room and beamed at Alit. 'Say something nice … if you like.'

Alit smiled. 'Well done?'

'I'll take rare over well done every time. Still.' She snatched up her umbrella. 'Come on! It's time to rescue Mr Grumpy-Beard from the hole he's in.'

'How are we going to do that?'

'Shh. Surprise, remember? But it might have something to do with the fact that I'm making it rain outside. Look!'

Alit stood on the chair and did so. Together, she and Missy stared out of the window as the first drops of water spattered the glass. Soon the rain was lashing the buildings and the ground below.

Missy took Alit's jacket and buttoned it over the top of Hunca Munca and Tom Thumb, then hid her own mouse under her purple coat. As she finished, she smiled at Alit. 'Now, while I go and brief Topknot on the plan, I have a very special mission for you. I need you to fetch something for me that we passed earlier. Are you up to the job?'

'Think so,' Alit said. 'Yeah!'

Missy went to kiss the little girl on the forehead and then cringed and shook her head. 'No. No. Yuck, how does he *do* this?'

The Master stood in the makeshift cell, his hands clasped behind his back. He was examining the ceiling for signs of an escape route when, behind him, the bolt on the door drew back. He spun round to find his future self, grinning at him lasciviously from the doorway.

'Need a hand?' she said.

The Master smiled and moved forward and Missy stepped aside to allow him out.

'Where are the Cybermen?'

'Distracted.' Missy started walking off. 'You coming?'

In the distance the sound of Cyber gunfire could be heard alongside crackling of electricity and strangled robotic cries.

'I used Topknot to cause a commotion, but he won't keep them busy for long.'

'You're quite good at this, aren't you?' the Master said approvingly.

Missy batted her eyelids at him. 'I'm a past Master!'

Just then Alit skidded round the corner ahead of them. She was not only wearing the black rubber boots she'd taken earlier – she was also carrying a pair of them in each hand.

'Oh.' The Master looked disappointed. 'I thought you'd used her as a distraction, too.'

'No. I had to send her on a very important mission. To get these.' Missy took the boots from Alit and proffered one pair to the Master.

He took them from her as if they were a brace of dead cats. 'Rubber boots?'

'Wellies!' Missy corrected him with a Celtic lilt.

'I do *not* wear "wellies"!'

'Come on! You know we always dress for the occasion.'

'I suppose you have something in mind.' The Master shook his head and sat down to pull on the pair of wellingtons. 'At least they're black.'

Once they were suitably booted, the three of them ran for the nearest exit that would lead them back to the bronzed railroad and a potential ride out of there. Outside the citadel of silos and warehouses, a torrential storm was pounding the metal plates of the deck. Missy opened her umbrella and the Master and Alit joined her beneath its protection, one either side. Then they strode out into the tempest.

'If this plan works, we'll have to say goodbye to Topknot,' Missy said.

'Easy come, easy go,' the Master replied. 'I just want to get out of here before more Cybermen arrive.'

'At least we found where the lift shafts are.' Missy gave Alit a smile. 'And if we know where they are on this deck, we can extrapolate where they are on Floor 507 and get back to the Doctor's TARDIS.'

'Hmmm.' The Master's face was inscrutable. 'So what is this amazing plan, then? Why the boots?'

Missy cocked an eyebrow and pointed upwards. 'Rain,' she said.

The Master gazed at the sky for a moment and then his face lit up, a broad smile spreading across his face. Then he laughed loudly. 'You'll be needing my laser screwdriver.'

'That would be nice,' Missy agreed.

Alit jumped as a group of Cybermen stepped out of cover behind them, their weapons firing. Explosions bloomed around her, and she screamed.

The Master produced his torch-like device and pointed it at the metal deck.

'That's it!' Missy called above the roar of rain and gunfire. 'Give the plan some welly!'

The Master blew her a kiss and fired the screwdriver. The electrical discharge hit the deck and arced away from the centre of impact, blowing out the lights and shorting the systems all around them.

The effect on the Cybermen was deadly. They stood, rooted to the spot as the flow of electricity reverberated through their bodies. The sections above their eyes where the lamps were exploded, and the Cybermen all fell to the ground save for the Leader. It managed to take a couple more steps towards Alit before tumbling face first to the floor.

The Master stopped firing and held the screwdriver aloft with a flourish.

Alit stared in shock at the fallen silver bodies around her. Even she knew that electricity and water did not mix. There had been a loose cable in the barn one day and the dripping water had caused the whole house to lose power. 'You electrocuted them!' she whispered, in some awe and not a little fear. Then she looked at her feet. 'And the boots saved us because they're rubber!'

'That about sums it up,' Missy agreed.

'That's really clever!'

Missy curtsied to Alit. 'Aren't I, just?'

They did not have to hitch a lift with a robo-tractor or cultivator. Instead, knowing that the produce from the arable farmland was delivered upstairs, they quickly located a conveyer belt system that was feeding bales of straw to the floors above – a simpler and much faster method of getting from one floor to another.

As they rode the enclosed escalator up through the heavens, the Master sat cross-legged with his eyes closed. Missy watched the golden fields and green citadel recede into the clouds below. Alit lay in the straw, marvelling at all they had done.

'You stopped the scarecrows sending their Cybermats,' she said. 'But what about stopping them?'

Missy glanced quickly at the Master and shook her head. 'It was just a wild idea. A long shot.' She mimed shaking someone's hand. 'One last hope.'

'But—'

Missy pushed an upright finger roughly against Alit's lips. 'Let's keep it to ourselves,' she whispered, 'shall we?'

Afraid now, Alit nodded.

When they reached Floor 507, the conveyer spilt its cargo out into a huge storage barn in the middle of nowhere. Robotic arms lifted the bales from the belt and stacked them. Beside the barn stood an extensive stable of horses and several carts. This would be how they returned to the farmstead, even if it might take a few days. They quickly harnessed one of the carts to a suitable horse and set off across the lush, green countryside, the Master taking the reins while Missy and Alit sat in the back.

'I wonder how the Doctor's injuries are,' Missy said conversationally.

'Who cares?' the Master answered, and it took him some time to break the silence that followed. 'Tell me. Travelling with the Doctor. What *is* that all about?'

'I was imprisoned. It was the only way out.'

'So you did have a plan before you ran into me. Get rid of him; betray him?' He licked his lips. 'Kill him?'

'Get rid …?' Missy looked at the Master, and her face became a stony façade. 'That has a certain ring to it.'

The Master smirked as he cracked the whip for the horse to move faster.

Missy turned away from him.

Alit eyed her, suspicious once more – especially as the woman now seemed to have a slightly distant, almost unhinged, look in her eye.

'Note to self: Get rid of … betray … kill.' Missy nodded. 'Yes. I suppose that's the only way.'